*Samuel French Acting Edition*

# Divorce Me, Darling

## by Alex Gottlieb

I0589019

‖SAMUEL FRENCH‖

**FOR PRODUCTION INQUIRIES**

UNITED STATES AND CANADA
info@concordtheatricals.com
1-866-979-0447

UNITED KINGDOM AND EUROPE
licensing@concordtheatricals.co.uk
020-7054-7200

Each title is subject to availability from Concord Theatricals Corp.,
depending upon country of performance. Please be aware that
*DIVORCE ME, DARLING* may not be licensed by Concord Theatricals
Corp. in your territory. Professional and amateur producers should
contact the nearest Concord Theatricals Corp. office or licensing
partner to verify availability.

Please refer to page 81 for further copyright information.

## STORY OF PLAY

A wink at women's lib, "Divorce Me, Darling" is the story of Amelia Conway, a highly successful divorce attorney in San Francisco who has insisted on using her maiden name while married for fifteen years to a highly successful construction engineer. He never forgets anniversaries, birthdays and holidays, but his roving work and roving eye keep his side of their double bed more unoccupied than occupied.

Amelia has never dreamed her marriage might become endangered, although she's been aware of her husband's casual affairs, until his new oversexed blonde secretary asks her to arrange an annulment so she can marry a married man. He is, of course, the motel-happy engineer.

Shall she give up the man she loves and simultaneously clip him of their community property as punishment for his philandering, or should she try to save the marriage by turning to a psychiatrist with a nervous tic and a yen for the blonde who turns men on faster than she can type?

Amelia finds the answer two hours and two hundred laughs later with the aid of a tape recorder and her young Machiavellian associate who is short in height but long in ideas.

3

# DESCRIPTION OF CHARACTERS

AMELIA CONWAY: Brilliant, beautiful divorce attorney in her late thirties or early forties. Wears expensive, good-taste clothes befitting her profession.

JONATHAN BENTLEY: Amelia's husband, a handsome, rugged construction engineer in his forties. He's in love with his wife, but he also loves to philander. He doesn't own a suit and rarely wears a tie.

TINA: Jonathan's new, oversexed secretary who wants an annulment of her unconsummated marriage so she can marry Jonathan. She's about twenty. Her skirts are high and her cleavage low.

ANDY: Amelia's young, fertile-minded associate. He's only five-feet-five but loves tall girls. Dresses like the Ivy League law school graduate that he is.

DR. FENWICK: A psychiatrist in his late thirties with a constant twitch because his patients make him nervous. His clothes are as costly as his office visits.

JULIE: Amelia's tall, long-legged secretary, a devout devotee of women's lib. She dresses like any well-dressed secretary in a lavish San Francisco law office.

MRS. HORTON: A rich, addle-pated divorcee in her thirties whose favorite indoor sport is hitting the bottle. Her wardrobe is good but on the flashy side.

# CAST OF CHARACTERS

*(In Order of Their Appearance)*

JULIE

ANDY

AMELIA CONWAY

TINA

JONATHAN BENTLEY

MRS. HORTON

DR. FENWICK

## SYNOPSIS OF SCENES

The entire action takes place in the San Francisco law offices of Amelia Conway. The time is the present.

## ACT ONE

SCENE 1: Nine-thirty in the morning.

SCENE 2: Four o'clock that afternoon.

SCENE 3: Two weeks later.

## ACT TWO

SCENE 1: Six o'clock that afternoon.

SCENE 2: An afternoon three weeks later.

# Divorce Me, Darling

## ACT ONE

### Scene 1

Scene: *The law office of* Amelia Conway. *The large modern desk and the high-backed leather chair behind it spell success and good taste. On the desk are a multi-line phone, an intercom, and a silver-framed picture of a rugged outdoor man in his late forties or early fifties. The other furniture—couch, chairs, coffee table, lamps—are in the same good taste. When the proper button is pressed, a shelf of law-books revolves to reveal a well-stocked bar.*

*The door or entryway to the outer office in Center Rear. Another door opens into a junior partner's office. The picture window behind the entryway reveals a balcony and a magnificent view of the Golden Gate Bridge.*

At Rise: Amelia's *secretary,* Julie, *enters with the morning mail. She is in her early twenties, quite tall, attractive, efficient. Entering directly behind her is* Andy. *He is five-feet-five, was graduated cum laude from Harvard Law School two years ago, and looks exactly like Robert Morse.*

Andy. Why? Why won't you go to bed with me?
Julie. I won't even discuss it at 9:30 in the morning.
Andy. When will you?

JULIE. Look, Andy, I admit your mind fascinates me.

ANDY. But my body doesn't?

JULIE. I'm one of the new breed of American women. Raised on vitamins and orange juice. We're five inches taller than our grandmothers.

ANDY. I think tall.

JULIE. I'll show you what I mean. Look into my eyes.

ANDY. (*Trying.*) I can't. (*Embittered.*) I told my mother a Harvard education wasn't enough.

JULIE. (*The phone rings. She answers.*) Miss Conway's office . . . No, but she should be here soon . . . One moment, please. (*Hand over receiver.*) New client. Wants a divorce in a hurry.

ANDY. They always do.

JULIE. She wants Amelia to handle her case personally.

ANDY. That's because she hasn't met me yet.

JULIE. (*Into phone.*) Could you come right over? . . . That'll be fine. (*Hangs up.*)

ANDY. Julie, do you think I'll ever be a success? I mean as a divorce attorney.

JULIE. Why specialize in such a limited field?

ANDY. Limited? How else could I meet so many sex-starved divorcees?

JULIE. Better not let Amelia hear that. You know her rule.

ANDY. I know. Don't play around with the clients.

JULIE. Or the secretaries in the office.

ANDY. Who's playing? I'm serious about you.

(*During the above,* AMELIA CONWAY, *briefcase in hand, enters through open doorway. She is in her early forties—a very smart, smartly-dressed career woman.*)

AMELIA. And I'm serious about office rules. (*Crosses to desk.*) Julie is out of bounds for you.

ANDY and JULIE. Good morning, Miss Conway.

AMELIA. Good morning. (*Sees letters.*) No anniversary present from my husband?

JULIE. Not in the mail.

AMELIA. Impossible. Jonathan never forgets. (*Picks up photograph.*) Good morning, darling. Where the hell's my anniversary present?

ANDY. Maybe he's too busy building that dam in the High Sierras.

AMELIA. (*Looks under letters.*) You positive there's no package for me?

JULIE. He probably sent it special delivery. That's always slower.

AMELIA. Never marry a construction engineer, Julie. He'll always be away somewhere. Building a mountain or tearing it down. Do you know he's been home for only six of our fifteen wedding anniversaries?

ANDY. That's still batting .400.

AMELIA. If a husband gave her a chance, every wife could bat a thousand. (*To* JULIE.) What's on the calendar?

JULIE. Mrs. Horton phoned after you left last night. She wants more alimony, both houses and all three cars.

ANDY. But Mr. Horton can have the children.

AMELIA. She'll get what she's entitled to and no more. A wife should leave her husband more than just his pride.

JULIE. And a Miss Tina Salisbury will be here any minute. She wants a divorce in a hurry.

AMELIA. *Miss* Salisbury? She really should get married first.

ANDY. I'll be glad to handle her case.

AMELIA. Harness your hormones, Andy. One of these days a nice rich girl about five-two will find you just her size.

ANDY. But I like tall girls. They're a challenge. Like Mount Everest. And my analyst says it's too late to change me. (*Outer office door opens Offstage.*)

JULIE. That may be your new client. (*She exits.*)

ANDY. Tell me something. What's the secret of a happy marriage?

AMELIA. Like mine? (ANDY *nods.*) It's hard to say. Fifteen years—and we're as crazy about each other as the day we eloped.

ANDY. I bet a lot of people said it wouldn't last.

AMELIA. I was the first.

(JULIE *enters, motions for* TINA SALISBURY *to enter. She's a knockout, in her early twenties.*)

JULIE. Miss Salisbury—Miss Conway. (*Exits.*)

AMELIA. Hello. (*Indicates* ANDY.) Mr. Ridgefield, my associate. (*Motions* TINA *to chair.*)

ANDY. (*Intrigued.*) How do you do.

TINA. Do what? (ANDY *and* AMELIA *watch wide-eyed while* TINA *sits down, crosses her legs and pulls her skirt down demurely.*)

AMELIA. I thought you liked tall girls.

ANDY. And short ones and middle-sized ones. Blondes, brunettes, redheads and albinos. That's my real problem.

AMELIA. The typical all-American boy. His office is right in there. And he has a load of work waiting for him.

ANDY. If you need me, just whistle. (*He exits backwards, fumbling for the door.*)

TINA. Why do men always stare at me?

AMELIA. You remind them of their mothers. Sit down, Miss Salisbury. It's really Mrs., isn't it?

TINA. (*Sitting.*) Mrs. Something. I never did get used to the name.

AMELIA. Or your husband either, apparently. Why do you want a divorce and I'll tell you why I'm against it?

TINA. Don't you believe in divorces?

AMELIA. Only as a source of income. For me.

TINA. Would you stay married to a man you'd known for only five weeks—and who's been stationed in Europe ever since?

AMELIA. How long is "ever since"?

TINA. Two years.

AMELIA. It took that long to find out you didn't love him?

TINA. No, I finally met a man I'm crazy about. My new boss.

AMELIA. Why do you think he'll marry you?

TINA. Why not?

AMELIA. (*Looks her over.*) I withdraw the question. Has he asked you to marry him?

TINA. Not in so many words.

AMELIA. There are only so many words. Four, to be exact. "Will you marry me?"

TINA. He's only waiting until my marriage is annulled—and you're the best divorce attorney in San Francisco. Do you know the stuffy California annulment laws?

AMELIA. By heart. (*Enumerating.*) Under the age of consent unless one or both parties cohabit after reaching that age. Unsound mind, unless they cohabit after coming to reason. Physical incapacity to cohabit. Fraud in obtaining consent, unless they cohabit after the party deceived learns of the fact. Force in obtaining consent, unless they cohabit afterwards. (*The saleswoman.*) Does anything there strike your fancy?

TINA. Well, we never did consummate the marriage. Not after the marriage, that is.

AMELIA. But you did before? (TINA *nods.*) You make an interesting point of law.

TINA. He was shipped out the morning after we drove back from Reno. Later I wrote him I wasn't going to have a baby, after all—and maybe we ought to call off the marriage.

AMELIA. What did he write back?

TINA. Just two words. "What marriage?"

AMELIA. Why don't I turn you over to Mr. Ridgefield? I think he'd like that.

TINA. You're the lawyer.

AMELIA. Thank you. I also get paid for my friendly little services. Don't you want to know how much they'll cost you?

TINA. Oh—nothing.

AMELIA. Nothing?

TINA. My boss will be glad to give me an annulment for a wedding present.

AMELIA. He sounds delightful. (*Into inter-com.*) Andy, could I bother you to come in here and— (*The door bursts open and* ANDY *enters.*)

ANDY. Sorry I kept you waiting.

AMELIA. (*To* TINA.) Never has his mind on anything but his work. (*To* ANDY.) Miss Salisbury—she has a married name but it escapes her—has a husband who needs annulling.

ANDY. My specialty. (*Indicating.*) Will you join me?

TINA. (*Rising.*) Thanks, Miss Conway. Or is it Mrs?

AMELIA. Sometimes I wonder.

ANDY. (*Follows* TINA.) This shouldn't take long. Just through the lunch hour. (*He exits after* TINA, *gives* AMELIA *an okay sign, closes door.*)

AMELIA. (*Into inter-com.*) Julie, would you come in, please?

JULIE. (*Offstage.*) Yes, Miss Conway.

(AMELIA *zips open her briefcase, starts to take out its contents.* JONATHAN BENTLEY *enters. He's a bronzed, muscular man who's lived outdoors most of his life. He carries two gift-wrapped packages and a large bouquet of flowers.*)

AMELIA. (*Not looking up.*) And please call Mrs. Horton and ask her to come in. I don't like the idea of a wife clipping her husband—even if I am her attorney.

JONATHAN. I'll make a note of that.

AMELIA. (*Happily, rises.*) Jonathan! What are you doing here? What happened to the damn dam?

JONATHAN. I put the concrete out to dry. I had to see you. (*He crosses to meet* AMELIA, *embraces her.*)

AMELIA. Careful! Don't crush my presents. They are for me, aren't they?

JONATHAN. And the flowers.

AMELIA. I was going to start divorce proceedings if I didn't hear from you by noon. (*Shakes package.*) What's in this one?

JONATHAN. Open it and see.

AMELIA. Anyone can do it that way. (*Unwrapping.*) Would you be bored if I told you I'm still in love with my husband?

JONATHAN. I'm really not good enough for you.

AMELIA. Of course you're not, but who can resist a man who never forgets an anniversary? (*She opens the box, takes out a stunning mink stole.*) Where's my candy?

JONATHAN. In the other package.

AMELIA. (*Kisses him.*) How long can you stay in town?

JONATHAN. Long enough.

AMELIA. That isn't what I meant.

JULIE. (*Enters with two vases.*) I thought you might need these.

AMELIA. (*To* JONATHAN.) That's what you should have—a secretary like Julie.

JONATHAN. I agree, but the ones you pick for me never look like her.

AMELIA. I'm not that foolish. (*Tosses stole to* JONATHAN, *takes vases.*) What do you think of a man who buys his wife a mink stole?

JULIE. It's beautiful, Mr. Bentley

JONATHAN. Would you like one?

AMELIA. Down, boy. You'd only hurt yourself.

JONATHAN. Maybe, but what a way to break a leg!

AMELIA. Back to your typewriter, Julie. He's been away from civilization too long. (JULIE *exits.* AMELIA *starts to put flowers into vases.*)

JONATHAN. Amelia, can we be serious for a minute?

AMELIA. I *am* serious.

JONATHAN. I left the job for a few days because I have something to tell you in person—not by letter or phone call. (*Turns* AMELIA, *holds her by shoulders.*) Can't you stop playing florist long enough to listen?

AMELIA. You *are* disturbed. All right, I'm listening. (*Indicates.*) This is my sympathetic ear and this is the shoulder you always cry on.

JONATHAN. You won't believe it, but I'm involved.

AMELIA. (*Her smile vanishes.*) I believe it.

JONATHAN. She's all mixed up. She wants me to marry her.

AMELIA. But that nasty little law against bigamy stands in the way?

JONATHAN. And you. You, Amelia.

AMELIA. Unless I decide to divorce you.

JONATHAN. (*He follows her while she places the vases of flowers.*) You don't understand. I thought it was just an affair. I never expected the girl to fall in love with me.

AMELIA. You can't blame her, can you? You are irresistible—especially those curly gray hairs on your chest. (*Pulls out hair and he winces.*) And you make so many promises that you can't keep.

JONATHAN. I swear I never said I'd marry her.

AMELIA. Did you say you wouldn't? (JONATHAN *makes a comme-ci comme-ca gesture.* AMELIA *pushes him into the chair in which* TINA *sat.*) Sit down. (*Indicates gifts.*) Candy—flowers—*and* a mink stole. You must really need help. How old is she?

JONATHAN. What is this—a cross-examination?

AMELIA. Just answer the question.

JONATHAN. Let's say she's old enough.

AMELIA. Let's say you've really flipped. What does she have—a father complex? Or did you lie about your age?

JONATHAN. You make me feel like I'm sitting in the electric chair.

AMELIA. You are.

JONATHAN. Well, maybe she is a little young for me and I might be a little old for her. But—

AMELIA and JONATHAN. —the chemistry's there.

JONATHAN. How are we going to handle this?

AMELIA. It's simple. Marry the girl. Walk into the sunset of life with her.

JONATHAN. (*Startled.*) Amelia! You're upset!

AMELIA. Upset? Why should I be upset? After all, I had the best fifteen years of your life. All this new girl wants are the dregs.

JONATHAN. What fifteen years? You've been wrapped up in your law practice and I've been working all over the world. How much time have we really spent together?

AMELIA. I loved every minute of it. I thought you did, too.

JONATHAN. Of course I did. Why do you think I've come to you for help?

AMELIA. The price is right. What's so special about this girl? I'm just asking for the record.

JONATHAN. All right, I'll be honest with you.

AMELIA. A first.

JONATHAN. She excites me. Morning, noon and night. Is that wrong?

AMELIA. Well, it does make for a long day. Is she more attractive than the little Eurasian number in Hong Kong?

JONATHAN. (*Surprised.*) How did you know about her?

AMELIA. She wrote and asked me to give you up. I wrote her my answer in a Chinese fortune cookie. And what about that Eskimo girl in Alaska?

JONATHAN. Sybil was not an Eskimo.

AMELIA. But you admit you melted a few igloos together.

JONATHAN. We just passed the time of day.

AMELIA. And the days were six months long. Have you got your heart set on this new girl? Without marriage, of course.

JONATHAN. Are you asking me if I love her?

AMELIA. I'll rephrase the question. Do you?

JONATHAN. I haven't had time to think about it. I've been too busy building a dam.

AMELIA. But you did find time for her. Even though we haven't seen each other for a month. (*Offers hand.*) Goodbye, Jonathan. I think we've finally had it.

JONATHAN. (*Taken aback.*) You're not going to help me?

AMELIA. No, Jonathan, I'm not. Happy anniversary. Happy wedding.

JONATHAN. But I don't want to marry Tina. I'm already married.

AMELIA. You remembered a little too late. (*Tardily.*) Did you say Tina?

JONATHAN. Tina Salisbury.

AMELIA. Tina Salisbury Something.

JONATHAN. How did you know?

AMELIA. Married once before to a soldier she hardly knew? A soldier shipped out before the marriage was consummated?

JONATHAN. (*Astounded.*) Don't tell me she came to you about an annulment?

AMELIA. She opened the store this morning. Smart girl—keeping it in the family. Were you planning to pay me with community property money?

JONATHAN. You're going to help her—not me?

AMELIA. In this case, I'm a lawyer first—a wife second.

JONATHAN. You're confused, Amelia. Why don't we have dinner tonight? We really should on our anniversary.

AMELIA. Like we always do? Every few years? No way!

JONATHAN. We'll talk about it when you get home tonight.

AMELIA. You're staying home while you're here? In our king-size bed?

JONATHAN. You're right. I'll go to a hotel.

AMELIA. Oh no, you stay. I can sleep in the guest room. I wouldn't want you to be uncomfortable while you're in town.

JONATHAN. I told Tina you were one in a million.

AMELIA. Where were you when you told her such a beautiful thought?

JONATHAN. Skiing.

AMELIA. Skiing? I couldn't even get you out to the movies. (*Shakes hands.*) Goodbye, Jonathan, and don't worry. Your girl has a most conscientious attorney.

JONATHAN. Goodbye, Amelia. I, hope you change your mind. And I hope the stole fits.

AMELIA. Like a noose. (*He exits.* AMELIA *fights back her tears, turns as* ANDY *enters from his office. He closes door.*)

ANDY. (*Pointing, shocked.*) Amelia, she wants to marry a married man.

AMELIA. I know.

ANDY. Yes, but do you know who the married man is?

AMELIA. I know that, too. I just gave him the air. (*Crosses to bar.*) I need a drink.

ANDY. You don't drink during the day.

AMELIA. I do now. (*She presses button. Bookshelf revolves, discloses circular bar.*)

ANDY. You must feel terrible.

AMELIA. Andy, what does he see in her, of course?

ANDY. Well, if you were a man his age with a wife—

AMELIA. (*Interrupting.*)  I know—my  age. And a girl her age told him she couldn't live without him—

ANDY. The divorce courts are full of these cases.

AMELIA. (*Downs her drink.*) How many drinks do I need before this doesn't seem important?

ANDY. I'm sure you can win him back.

AMELIA. But do I want him back? And if I do, do I get him back on my terms or his?

ANDY. Why don't I ask Dr. Fenwick this afternoon?

AMELIA. What would your analyst know? He's a bachelor, isn't he?

ANDY. Only recently. His wife went to another analyst and found out her husband didn't understand her.

AMELIA. Why didn't we handle the divorce?

ANDY. She went the Vegas routine. And married her analyst thirty minutes later.

AMELIA. She really went from couch to couch.

ANDY. (*At bar.*) Another drink?

AMELIA. I shouldn't.

ANDY. It'll give you courage.

AMELIA. Or make me cry.

(MRS. HORTON *enters, followed by* JULIE. MRS. HORTON *is an attractive, high-strung society matron in her early thirties.*)

JULIE. You can't break in like this, Mrs. Horton.

AMELIA. It's all right, Julie. When a client is disturbed, we waive office protocol. (JULIE *sighs, exits.*)

MRS. HORTON. Amelia, I've never been so upset. (*To* ANDY.) Could I have a drink, please? I have a terrible hangover.

ANDY. What gave it to you?

MRS. HORTON. My husband—the one I'm divorcing —did it to me last night.

AMELIA. Did what, Mrs. Horton? (MRS. HORTON *takes a drink from* ANDY, *downs it.*) I said did what, Mrs. Horton?

MRS. HORTON. Can I still get a divorce after what happened?

ANDY. (*To* MRS. HORTON.) Did what?

AMELIA. Weren't you and your husband supposed to have a reconciliation meeting last night?

MRS. HORTON. We did. (*To* ANDY.) Could I have a refill, please?

ANDY. Why not? I got straight "A's" in bartending at Harvard.

AMELIA. Go on, Mrs. Horton.

MRS. HORTON. I told Oliver no reconciliation. All I wanted was my happiness and all the money and all the cars.

AMELIA. Did he get angry?

MRS. HORTON. No, he just kept smiling and refilling my glass. And you know I don't drink. (*Takes drink from* ANDY, *empties it.*)

AMELIA. I can see that.

MRS. HORTON. I was in no condition to drive so he said he'd take me home. But he didn't. He took me to a motel!

ANDY. Why didn't you put up an argument?

MRS. HORTON. I've always wanted to see what it was like in a motel.

AMELIA. That makes two of us. What is the difference?

ANDY. You have to put quarters in the radio. (AMELIA *and* MRS. HORTON *stare at him.*) I read that somewhere.

MRS. HORTON. (*To* AMELIA.) You told me not to, but I was unfaithful with my own husband.

AMELIA. I'd settle for that.

MRS. HORTON. Amelia, you don't know what it means to have a husband who plays around.

AMELIA. Don't I? Did yours ever come home and tell you he was in love with one of his conquests?

MRS. HORTON. (*Indignantly.*) He wouldn't dare! I'm the only woman he ever loved. The others were just—

AMELIA. (*Interrupting.*) That's what I'm trying to

say. I knew a woman whose husband was a construction engineer, like mine. She suspected he had an occasional girl friend.

MRS. HORTON. I hope she did something about it.

AMELIA. No, she cared for him too much to let a casual physical affair come between them.

MRS. HORTON. And they're still happily married?

AMELIA. Just celebrated their fifteenth anniversary.

MRS. HORTON. I don't know who this stupid woman is, but she's more broad-minded than I am. Maybe she's afraid she can't get another man.

AMELIA. Maybe.

MRS. HORTON. I'll bet her husband wouldn't dream of taking her to a motel.

AMELIA. She's not the type.

ANDY. Perhaps she ought to be.

MRS. HORTON. (*To* AMELIA.) Well, that's her problem. What does last night with Oliver do to my divorce case?

AMELIA. I wasn't there, of course, but it appears there was condonation on your part.

ANDY. That's conditional forgiveness of the original offense constituting the cause for divorce.

AMELIA. In simpler words, you restored the offending to conjugal rights.

MRS. HORTON. That's simpler words?

AMELIA. Your case is like Hamburger v. Hamburger (1943) or Comfort v. Comfort—now there's a nice homey name—Comfort—(1941) or Cassidy v. Cassidy (1883).

MRS. HORTON. Husbands were cheating that far back?

ANDY. Well, not in motels.

MRS. HORTON. Well, then, how do I uncondone Oliver?

AMELIA. Condonation is revoked and the original course for divorce is revived by a new act. By another conjugal unkindness.

ANDY. That means you have to catch Oliver at it again.

AMELIA. The law's the law.

MRS. HORTON. I'll tell him at lunch today. Now I'm sorry I picked such a homely new secretary for him.

ANDY. (*Offers refilled glass.*) One for the road?

MRS. HORTON. Thanks, but I'm driving. (*Downs drink.*) I don't recommend motels. Not with the radio playing. Too many commercials. (*She exits unsteadily.*)

ANDY. I promised to take your new client to lunch. Any instructions?

AMELIA. Go see your analyst like you always do. I'll take her. (*Jaw set.*) Now that I know who she is and what she's done to my miserable married life—

ANDY. (*Hurries to stop her.*) No, Amelia. Count to a thousand first.

AMELIA. Don't worry, I'm not the hair-pulling type. I just want to ask her one question.

ANDY. Like "Why don't you drop dead?"

AMELIA. No, I want to ask her what she sees in that lecherous old man. (*She starts for* ANDY'S *office, sees mink stole, drapes it over her shoulders.*) I might as well wear my Good Conduct Medal. (*Exits into* ANDY'S *office.*)

BLACKOUT

*CURTAIN*

ACT ONE

SCENE 2

SCENE: *The same.*

AT RISE: *It is four p.m. of same day.* JULIE, *one foot on coffee table, is straightening her pants suit.*

ANDY *enters. He carries a tall stack of law books.*
*Each volume has several bookmarks in it.*)

ANDY. Do you mind if I watch and get a double
hernia?

JULIE. Like my new outfit?

ANDY. Pants suits and bucket seats are a girl's best
friend.

JULIE. I'll give you a hint how to get somewhere
with me.

ANDY. I know. Grow.

JULIE. No, I get mellow when I drink. At least,
that's the excuse I give myself.

ANDY. The bar is officially open.

JULIE. Put those down before you strain yourself.

ANDY. (*Crosses to desk.*) I've been doing research for
Amelia's counter-suit. (*Piles up books.*) You'll never
believe how many husbands start fooling around after
fifteen years of marriage. They don't all get divorced,
of course. A lot stay together on account of the
children. Usually children they detest.

JULIE. There must be a better way for a man and
woman to live together.

ANDY. Our generation has found it. They simply live
together. Did Amelia say when she'd be back?

JULIE. No, but her husband phoned a dozen times.
He's furious about something.

ANDY. Did he give you any clues?

JULIE. Only one. He said, "Well, it's three o'clock.
The double-crossing bitch can't do any more damage
today."

ANDY. When he said "bitch", was he referring to
Amelia or to Tina?

JULIE. I'm sure he meant our boss.

ANDY. I hope she gets here before Dr. Fenwick.

JULIE. You called in your analyst?

ANDY. (*Goes behind bar, mixes an involved con-
coction from several bottles.*) Amelia won't go to his

office, so he's coming here after he shrinks his last head today. Besides, he wants to meet you.

JULIE. Why?

ANDY. He's intrigued by my dreams about you.

JULIE. How have you been doing?

ANDY. I'm exhausted when I wake up. (*Offers drink.*) Here. I know you didn't take your coffee break today. (*He hides drink under bar as outer office door offstage opens and slams shut.* JONATHAN *enters.*)

JONATHAN. (*Seething.*) Where is she? Where's my two-timing wife—the lady bank thief!

ANDY. He still loves her.

JULIE. She's not back yet, Mr. Bentley.

JONATHAN. She's hiding from me. (*Crosses to* ANDY'S *office, looks in.*) Amelia! Come out of there and face me man-to-man!

ANDY. You seem upset. (*Brings glass above bar.*) Have a drink.

JONATHAN. I could use one. (*Drinks it down, almost chokes.*) My God! What did you put in there?

ANDY. It's a Radcliffe Special. At Harvard we used to order it as a final desperate measure.

JONATHAN. Do you know where Amelia's been all afternoon? (ANDY *and* JULIE *shake their heads.*) There's no excuse for what she did. Just because she thinks I'm making a fool of myself.

ANDY. Are you?

JONATHAN. Are I what?

ANDY. Making a fool of yourself?

JONATHAN. You met Tina.

JULIE. (*Honestly.*) Does she love you like Amelia does?

JONATHAN. Amelia? We've been drifting apart ever since she bought that king-size bed.

ANDY. Marriages aren't made in bed.

JONATHAN. Maybe not, but it's a damned good meeting place for a husband and wife.

JULIE. Why are you so angry? Because Amelia isn't wild about your fiancee?

JONATHAN. You should hear the things she told Tina about me!

ANDY. Well, it wasn't exactly hearsay evidence.

JONATHAN. There are certain facts about a man that a new wife should find out for herself.

JULIE. Does Tina still want to marry you?

JONATHAN. More than ever. She says no man could be as miserable as Amelia painted me. Tina loves me for me—not for my money.

JULIE. You could have fooled me.

JONATHAN. That's why Amelia did what she did this afternoon.

ANDY. What did she did?

JULIE. Or do you want us to guess?

JONATHAN. I'll tell you. What's the first thing a man does when he's engaged to a girl?

JULIE. Tell his wife?

JONATHAN. No, he buys her an engagement ring. Nothing fancy. Just a simple little diamond.

ANDY. How simple?

JONATHAN. Six thousand dollars. I wrote the jeweler a check and he phoned to see if the check was all right. It wasn't.

JULIE. But your joint checking account is loaded.

JONATHAN. *Was* loaded. The jeweler apologized, said something about "insufficient funds," and pulled the ring off Tina's finger. Nearly broke it.

ANDY. What a shame Amelia wasn't there.

JONATHAN. I went right over to the Bank of America to tear it apart. Branch by branch. How much—just how much money do you think Amelia left in our account?

ANDY. Five dollars?

JONATHAN. One dollar! One lousy, stinking, devaluated dollar.

JULIE. (*To* ANDY.) Remind me to have a joint account when I get married.

JONATHAN. I knew Amelia was up to something when she said we ought to have joint accounts because I'd be out of town so much.

ANDY. When did she say that?

JONATHAN. On our honeymoon.

JULIE. What about your savings account? You have a good balance there.

JONATHAN. I *did*. Amelia emptied that, too. And the safety deposit box. What do you think she left there?

ANDY. Her fingerprints?

JONATHAN. My will. And a note saying, "You'll have to change this yourself, darling. I've taken care of everything else." You're damned right she has! I'm dead broke. I don't even have enough money to take Tina to dinner. (AMELIA, *her arms loaded with pack-ages, enters in time to hear* JONATHAN'S *last remark.*)

AMELIA. Use a credit card. You can write the tip on the check.

JONATHAN. (*Caustically.*) What do I use for taxi money?

AMELIA. (*Hands packages to* JULIE *and* ANDY, *opens her purse.*) Here's five dollars. I'll give you another five tomorrow.

JONATHAN. (*Spurns money.*) You won't get away with this, Amelia!

AMELIA. Oh, I think I will. I've got a great lawyer. She said I'd feel better if I went shopping.

JULIE. Looks like you bought everything you saw. (*Exits with packages.*)

AMELIA. Only the things I didn't need. You'd better put them in the other office, Andy. They seem to make Jonathan nervous.

ANDY. (*Starts out.*) They do feel expensive.

JONATHAN. Hold it, Junior! I want to see what the spendthrift bought!

AMELIA. Oh, wait and see my new mink coat. They're sending it home.

JONATHAN. You bought a mink coat!

AMELIA. To keep my other one company. They practically gave it away. Six thousand dollars.

ANDY. Wear it on your third finger, left hand. (*Exits.*)

JONATHAN. The coat goes back, Amelia, and don't argue with me. Now what about our stocks and bonds? Where are they?

AMELIA. In the safety deposit box, of course.

JONATHAN. Oh, no, they're not! I looked.

AMELIA. Not in my new one. They seem happier there.

JONATHAN. You always said you didn't believe in wives clipping their husbands when their marriages broke up. What happened?

AMELIA. I decided it didn't apply to me.

JONATHAN. There's a community property law in California. Heaven knows you've quoted it enough.

AMELIA. There's one part I never quoted to you, darling. A few years ago the courts could have awarded me *all* the community property—one hundred per cent of it—*if*.

JONATHAN. If what?

AMELIA. If I could prove you committed adultery.

JONATHAN. (*Outraged.*) I slept with the girl I'm going to marry. Since when is that adultery? (ANDY *and* JULIE *enter.*)

ANDY. Did we miss anything you want us to swear to in court?

AMELIA. No, this is going to be a friendly divorce.

JONATHAN. You call emptying my bank accounts friendly?

AMELIA. Julie, write Mr. Bentley a check for a hundred dollars.

JONATHAN. A hundred dollars? Tina spends that much just looking in windows.

JULIE. What shall I charge it to?

AMELIA. Depreciation. (JULIE *exits.* JONATHAN *stares at* ANDY.)

ANDY. I can't think of a single excuse to leave.

AMELIA. (*To* JONATHAN.) Where's Tina now? I thought you two were inseparable.

JONATHAN. She's at Magnin's. I told her to go shopping while I went to the bank. (*The inter-com buzzer sounds.* AMELIA *crosses to desk, flips down key.*)

AMELIA. Yes, Julie?

JULIE'S VOICE. (*From inter-com.*) Miss Salisbury is on the phone. For your husband.

AMELIA. (*Offers phone to* JONATHAN.) A zipper must be stuck.

JONATHAN. (*Takes phone.*) Hello, darling, are you enjoying yourself? . . . I'm sure it's beautiful. What else did you buy? . . . And what else? . . . And what else?

AMELIA. (*To* ANDY.) She's crazy about his body and his bank account, but not in that order.

JONATHAN. (*Into phone.*) Of course I have the money. Tell them to charge everything to me. (*To* AMELIA, *hand over mouthpiece.*) You didn't close our charge accounts, did you?

AMELIA. Every one.

JONATHAN. (*Into phone.*) Tell them to hold everything on the layaway plan. I'll see you at the hotel, baby. (*Interrupts.*) Goodbye, Tina. I'm talking from the camp of the enemy. (*He hangs up.*)

AMELIA. (*Sweetly.*) You've had a bad day, haven't you, baby?

JONATHAN. Why didn't you throw Tina out of your office?

AMELIA. Why didn't you throw her out of your bed?

JULIE'S VOICE. You can't go in now, Mrs. Horton. She's in conference.

MRS. HORTON. (*Enters. Highly perturbed.*) Thank goodness my lawyers are here. I rushed right over from lunch.

ANDY. Lunch at four o'clock?

MRS. HORTON. My husband likes to linger over

dessert. And a few martinis. (*Eyes* JONATHAN.) I don't believe we've met.

AMELIA. Mr. Bentley—Mrs. Horton. He's the construction engineer I told you about.

MRS. HORTON. The one with a you-know-what in every port?

AMELIA. The one. And happily married for fifteen years.

JONATHAN. I don't know what Amelia's been telling you, but we're getting divorced.

MRS. HORTON. You're lucky. I can't because I lost my head last night.

AMELIA. We told you what to tell your husband.

MRS. HORTON. I did, but he refuses to cheat on me again.

AMELIA. There's a man for you.

MRS. HORTON. Couldn't you call that a conjugal unkindness?

AMELIA. Well, it would be a legal precedent.

MRS. HORTON. I was so mad I told him I was moving out. I can't bear to spend another night with him.

AMELIA. So *he* agreed to move out.

MRS. HORTON. No, he promised to buy me my own motel. He says I'm a different woman in a motel.

ANDY. You really have a problem.

AMELIA. Some problem. (*Looks at* JONATHAN.) A husband who's still crazy about his wife—even though he wanders off the reservation from time to time.

MRS. HORTON. He doesn't really care for me. It's just that he breaks out in a rash when I mention the words "community property." (JONATHAN *absentmindedly begins to scratch himself.*)

AMELIA. Do you want my advice?

MRS. HORTON. Of course I do.

AMELIA. Look in the yellow pages for a reliable real estate broker. Find a little twenty-room unit overlooking the Bay, put up a "No Vacancy" sign, and live happily ever after in all twenty rooms.

MRS. HORTON. What a tempting idea! Sneaking away from the children every night.

AMELIA. Sleep on it and let me know what you decide.

MRS. HORTON. Thanks, Amelia. (*To* JONATHAN.) You've got a fine lawyer, Mr. Bentley. Take her advice. If she says no divorce, no divorce.

JONATHAN. I'll keep it in mind. (MRS. HORTON *exits.*)

AMELIA. Don't bother, Jonathan. My advice to you is just the opposite.

JONATHAN. (*Puzzled.*) The opposite?

ANDY. (*Indicates books on desk.*) After all my hours of research?

AMELIA. I've decided that Jonathan and Tina deserve each other. (*To* JONATHAN.) You can give her everything she's never had—and she can give you your first heart attack.

JONATHAN. (*Insulted.*) I happen to be in great condition.

AMELIA. You keep saying that when they put you in the oxygen tent. (ANDY *follows their conversation like he's watching a tennis match.*)

JONATHAN. Don't change the subject. How am I going to pay for Tina's annulment?

AMELIA. Consider it my wedding present. That's the least I can do for a man who spends most of his life passing himself off as a bachelor.

JONATHAN. You're a fine one to talk. For fifteen years you've insisted on using your maiden name. Why? Why did you have to be Miss Conway and not Mrs. Bentley?

AMELIA. I was Mrs. Bentley where it counted.

JONATHAN. You invented women's lib before they had a name for it.

AMELIA. I haven't had much libbing lately.

JONATHAN. Now tell me you're against man's lib.

AMELIA. You mean libido.

JONATHAN. What's wrong with my libido?

AMELIA. Don't ask me—ask Tina. You'll have her until she makes an old man out of you. About next November.

ANDY. I've just become anti-marriage.

AMELIA. So am I. I got more warmth out of my electric blanket the last two years.

JONATHAN. If you mean that, then I'm not hurting you.

AMELIA. (*Not meaning it.*) Hurting me? You're giving me what I never had—my freedom.

JONATHAN. What do you expect to do with it?

AMELIA. My type happens to be in great demand. For all you know, I've been having a ball.

JONATHAN. (*Amused.*) Not you, Amelia. I know you better than that.

AMELIA. Do you? Andy!

ANDY. Here I am. Right here.

AMELIA. (*Crosses to desk, takes key out of drawer.*) Open my private file and bring me the letters I got from Mr. X.

ANDY. Mr. —? (*Gets it.*) Oh, Mr. X! You can't show those to anyone!

AMELIA. Why not?

JONATHAN. He's damned right you can't. And you know why? Because they don't exist.

AMELIA. Oh, no? Get the letters, Andy.

ANDY. All of them?

AMELIA. Maybe they are too strong to take in one dose. Get the one dated December 17th. The one that starts out, "My one, my own, my darling Amelia."

ANDY. "Et cetera, et cetera, *et cetera!*"

JONATHAN. Translate "et cetera." Especially that last one.

AMELIA. You just said you didn't believe me.

JONATHAN. I still don't, but I want to see it. (*Sits down, to* ANDY.) I'll wait right here while you write it.

ANDY. Won't take me a minute (*He exits.*)

JONATHAN. What a con act! You want me to believe you've been doing what I've been doing.

AMELIA. What have you been doing, darling?

JONATHAN. You know damned well what I've been doing.

AMELIA. And what makes you think a married woman can't enjoy herself like her husband does?

JONATHAN. Maybe some women, but not you, Amelia. I know better. (ANDY *enters, carrying a letter.*)

ANDY. Well, that didn't take long, did it?

AMELIA. (*To* JONATHAN.) Shall I read to you—like I always do when you're tired?

JONATHAN. (*Rising.*) I'm never tired any more. (*Crosses to* ANDY.) You sure you want me to read this?

AMELIA. I should be ashamed of what I did, but go ahead. Maybe you'll believe me then.

JONATHAN. You never give up, do you? (*Takes letter, reads.*) "My one, my own, my darling Amelia. The memory of last night is still on my lips and in my arms. From the moment we drove up to the cabin in the moonlight and I carried you in . . ." (*He continues to read silently, eyes widening, finally looks up, outraged.*) He's a sex maniac!

AMELIA. Don't knock it.

JONATHAN. Amelia, how could you!

AMELIA. I guess I was frustrated.

JONATHAN. Frustrated, hell! This letter proves what you accused me of—adultery!

AMELIA. It didn't seem like it at the time.

JONATHAN. It will to a judge. (*Brandishes letter.*) Now we'll see who gets the community property. You've been women's adlibbing—that's what you've been doing. (ANDY *grabs letter.* JONATHAN *starts after him, but* AMELIA *bars his way.*) You give me that letter! It's evidence.

AMELIA. It's evidence I'm quite a woman.

JONATHAN. Okay, keep it. But I warn you—don't

burn that letter. Or the rest of your love life. I'm going
to subpoena your files.

AMELIA. My pleasure. (JULIE *enters with a check.*)

JULIE. Will you sign this, Miss Conway?

AMELIA. Of course. We can't expect a big strapping
man like Mr. Bentley to live on love. (*Crosses to desk,
signs check with pen* ANDY *hands her.*) Unless he's
too proud to take the money.

JONATHAN. Proud? It's my money, isn't it? (*To*
ANDY.) Who's Mr. X? I'll make it worth your while.
I'll make you vice president of five corporations.

AMELIA. Don't listen to him, Andy. I happen to be
the biggest stockholder and I'm thinking of firing the
president. (*Offers check to* JONATHAN.) Here, darling.
Live it up.

JONATHAN. Who's Mr. X?

AMELIA. Why, Jonathan, you actually sound jealous.

JONATHAN. (*Airily.*) Jealous? With a girl like Tina
waiting for me? (*Takes check.*) Thanks for nothing.
(*Starts out.*)

JULIE. Dr. Fenwick is here to see you, Miss Conway.

AMELIA. Dr. Fenwick?

ANDY. My analyst. He's going to help you as a
personal favor to me.

AMELIA. Who needs a psychiatrist?

JONATHAN. You need somebody to straighten you
out.

AMELIA. You don't? Your libido's gone to your head.
(*To* JULIE.) Please ask him to come in. (JULIE *exits.*)

JONATHAN. (*At door.*) You going to tell him about
you and Mr. X?

AMELIA. (*Nods.*) And you and Miss S.

JONATHAN. Psychiatrists are a menace. They ought
to be allowed to listen to each other and no one else.

(DR. FENWICK *enters. He's in his thirties, wears shell-
    rimmed glasses and has a decided tic.*)

DR. FENWICK. How do you do. I didn't mean to
barge in. (*Tics violently.*)

JONATHAN. Don't be nervous, Doc.

DR. FENWICK. Who's nervous? (*Tics again.*)

JONATHAN. (*Indicates* AMELIA.) You've got yourself a beaut, Doc. She's a happily married woman, but the way she's been carrying on!

DR. FENWICK. With you?

JONATHAN. (*Tics.*) Of course not. (*Tics again.*) I'm her husband. (*He exits.*)

DR. FENWICK. (*Looks after him.*) Poor fellow. He needs treatment. (*Tics violently, turns to* AMELIA.) You must be Miss Conway.

AMELIA. I really don't know why Andy asked you to come here. I'm the best adjusted woman I know.

ANDY. You won't be after Dr. Fenwick gets through with you. (*Holds up letter.*) I better put this back in Mrs. Gunderson's file.

AMELIA. Wasn't I brilliant to remember her first name was Amelia?

ANDY. Who was Mr. X? You never did tell me.

AMELIA. Mrs. Gunderson never told me, either. But he must have been quite a guy. (ANDY *exits.*)

DR. FENWICK. Fine boy your associate, Miss Conway. He's sick.

AMELIA. Sick?

DR. FENWICK. Well, not really sick—just *sick.* (*Tics violently.*)

AMELIA. Have you ever thought of getting your shirts a size larger?

DR. FENWICK. Oh, don't let my tic bother you. The stories I have to listen to upset me.

AMELIA. Then why be a psychiatrist?

DR. FENWICK. I was going to be a surgeon— (*Demonstrates.*) but my hands were always shaking.

AMELIA. Be a psychiatrist. You really think it would help to talk about Jonathan and me?

DR. FENWICK. It's the best way to probe into the reasons for the break-up of your marriage.

AMELIA. Yes, but when we're through, will I get him back or will I just know why I'm a rejected wife?

DR. FENWICK. Maybe both. Why don't we talk about it as long as I'm here?

AMELIA. I'll try anything. Do we start when I was a little girl? Or can we skip the preliminaries?

DR. FENWICK. No point being formal. Lie down on the couch.

AMELIA. Lie down on the couch?

DR. FENWICK. I think better with my patient in that position.

AMELIA. I don't. I talk better on my feet. You know, pacing up and down the courtroom.

DR. FENWICK. (*Disturbed.*) That does pose a problem. I find it hard to listen with an empty couch in the room.

AMELIA. All right then, *you* lie down.

DR. FENWICK. (*Tic-ing.*) I don't know if I should. It's highly irregular.

AMELIA. So are a lot of things that are happening to me. (*Pats couch.*) Go ahead. Try it for size.

DR. FENWICK. Frankly, many's the time I've felt like saying "move over" to some of my patients. (*Tics.*) I needed the rest more than they did.

AMELIA. (*Helps him onto couch.*) Well, you rest now, Doctor, while I unburden myself.

DR. FENWICK. (*Relaxing.*) Say, it is nice. I must do this more often.

AMELIA. I'll begin at the end and sort of sum up everything. Would that be all right?

DR. FENWICK. Not according to the textbooks, but it's your life.

AMELIA. (*Paces.*) Well, my husband's had a roving eye for God knows how many years. I didn't mind in the beginning because that's how I met him. But now he's fallen in love—or thinks he has—with a fine physical specimen in her early twenties.

DR. FENWICK. Do you really want to let him go?

AMELIA. I'm not sure. What do you think?

DR. FENWICK. We're not paid to think.

AMELIA. I suppose what I really want is to teach him a lesson. And then get him back. But on my terms.

DR. FENWICK. You're walking a tightwire.

AMELIA. How is that?

DR. FENWICK. What if you drive him into actually marrying this girl?

AMELIA. Then he hasn't any more brains than his secretary. (*Caustically.*) *Secretary?* I bet she can't even take shorthand.

DR. FENWICK. Roving husbands aren't looking for brains or shorthand experts.

AMELIA. (*Looks in mirror.*) I admit she has it all over me—except in brains. (*Turns away as she talks.*) Today—in self-defense—I told him I've been carrying on with a nonexistent Mr. X. It seems to me he showed a glimmer of jealousy. Not much, but a glimmer. Jonathan doesn't seem to like the idea of his wife in another man's arms, but I think he likes even less the idea of giving up his new girl. (*Turns to couch.*) Tell me, Doctor, what's my problem? (*She discovers* DR. FENWICK *has just closed his eyes, curled up and gone to sleep. He smiles, snores loudly.*)

## BLACKOUT

## *CURTAIN*

## ACT ONE

### SCENE 3

SCENE: *The same.*

AT RISE: *It is two weeks later. At the desk* JULIE *is sorting the mail. She looks up as* AMELIA *enters. She is obviously low in spirits.*

JULIE. You don't look like you're getting much help from Dr. Twitch.

AMELIA. Two or three times a week for two weeks, and all he has on his pad are doodles of Tina—nude.

JULIE. Are you sleeping better since you started to see him?

AMELIA. Have you ever slept in a king-size bed?

JULIE. Not alone.

AMELIA. You can roll around for hours and never run across anybody.

JULIE. Why don't you buy an Army cot?

AMELIA. Not until I'm sure I've lost Jonathan for keeps. Not until Tina's annulled and he's divorced.

JULIE. You know what you're doing, Miss Conway?

AMELIA. Committing hari-kari?

JULIE. You're joining the club of women who knew they were right—and lost their husbands to prove it. It's a big club. (*The outer office door opens and closes offstage.*) That must be Tina baby. She phoned that she had to see you.

AMELIA. What's she doing in town?

JULIE. Your husband's lawyer in Reno advised him not to have her work in his office while her annulment proceedings were pending.

AMELIA. Office? He's got a 2 x 4 shack where they're building the dam. She'd have to take dictation—among other things—standing up.

JULIE. I'm only repeating what she told me.

AMELIA. Okay, send her in. After all, she is my client.

JULIE. Do you want Andy to join you?

AMELIA. All he'll do is stare at her legs, but ask him to come in. ·

JULIE. (*Crosses to door.*) As soon as he gets back from Dr. Fenwick.

AMELIA. I hope he's helping Andy more than he is me.

JULIE. (*Indicates.*) Why don't you use your tape

recorder and save the money? I bet you could analyze yourself just as well.

AMELIA. No, he's really good. He's a fascinating listener.

JULIE. Is that all he does? Just listen?

AMELIA. And doodle. He's having another analyst analyze them.

JULIE. No wonder psychiatrists charge so much. It's the only way they can afford each other.

AMELIA. How does Andy manage to pay?

JULIE. His mother sends him the money. That's his problem.

AMELIA. And Dr. Fenwick says Andy won't be adjusted until he's free of his mother. But he can't get free of her until he completes his analysis—and he needs his mother's money for that. It's a vicious circle.

JULIE. What's the answer?

AMELIA. Marry a rich girl and use *her* mother's money. In the meantime, send in my oversexed client. (JULIE *exits.* AMELIA *looks at* JONATHAN'S *picture on the desk.*) Go ahead! Wreck your prostate ten years ahead of time. (*Looks up as* TINA *enters.*) Nice to see you. How are my husband and your lover?

TINA. He's fine. How's Mr. X?

AMELIA. (*Pleased.*) Jonathan told you about him?

TINA. First he said there was no such fellow. Then he said if there was, he'd wring his neck. Johnny's very nervous these days.

AMELIA. Must be about some trouble at the bank.

TINA. I came here to find out what's holding up my annulment.

AMELIA. Didn't that old thing go through yet?

TINA. Where's Andy? Nothing personal, Miss Conway, but he seems to know what's going on here.

AMELIA. Can I do anything for you until he gets back?

TINA. I'm not sure. Can I trust you, Miss Conway?

AMELIA. Of course. We have a client-attorney relationship. Nothing you tell Andy or me can be used against you.

TINA. Well, it's about my engagement ring. Johnny promised me one, but now—out of the clear blue—he's against engagement rings. He says if two people are engaged, they know it and that's all that matters.

AMELIA. Oh, I agree with him. Why tell the whole world about your happiness?

TINA. Then there's the mink coat.

AMELIA. He promised you a mink coat?

TINA. To celebrate our first month of going together. Now he says mink is ostentatious. In bad taste.

AMELIA. He's right. Only minks wear them nowadays. You insist on chinchilla. He'll love you all the more for it. (*There's a knock on the door.*) Come in.

ANDY. (*Enters with* DR. FENWICK.) It's Wednesday and Dr. Fenwick doesn't play golf, so he thought he'd drop by in case you wanted to see him today.

DR. FENWICK. (*To* AMELIA.) You're not the easiest woman to find time with alone.

AMELIA. I told you before, my couch is your couch. (*Makes introductions.*) Miss Salisbury—Dr. Fenwick.

TINA. Hello.

DR. FENWICK. (*Impressed, tics.*) Hello! (*To* ANDY.) Why don't I wait in your office?

AMELIA. I'll go with you. It's cosier in there, and Miss Salisbury can talk to Andy in here.

DR. FENWICK. Fine. (*To* TINA.) You're a rare type. (*Tics.*) I can tell by the way you talk.

TINA. All I said was "hello."

DR. FENWICK. It expressed your entire character. (*Tics energetically, escorts* AMELIA *out, turns back in doorway.*) You must come up to my office sometime and see my doodles. (*Exits into* ANDY'S *office.*)

TINA. (*Indicates door.*) Andy, is that him?

ANDY. Is who who?

TINA. Dr. Fenwick. Is he Mr. X?

ANDY. Is he Mr. —? (*Admiringly.*) Say, you are perceptive! How did you figure that out?

TINA. Did you see the way he looked at her?

ANDY. I told him he shouldn't meet her so openly.

TINA. She's pretty careless herself. Saying "my couch is your couch." Trying to make a gag out of it.

ANDY. She didn't fool you, did she?

TINA. Women have an instinct about those things. Is he really a doctor?

ANDY. He's an analyst. A psychiatrist.

TINA. You know something? I've never been out with one.

ANDY. You know, I think you *could* tell Dr. Fenwick things. Like—would you marry Jonathan if he weren't loaded?

TINA. Oh, I doubt if I'd marry a man his age just for love.

ANDY. (*Astonished.*) Would you repeat that?

TINA. I said I doubt if I'd marry a man his age just for love.

ANDY. Tina, do you know what you're saying?

TINA. Sure I do, but you can't tell Johnny.

ANDY. I can't?

TINA. No, there's a confidential relationship between a client and her attorney.

ANDY. I didn't realize we were representing a law student.

TINA. Miss Conway told me that, so I might as well tell you the truth as long as it can't hurt me.

ANDY. All right, why did you get married before?

TINA. The first or second or third time?

ANDY. You've been married three times? (*He walks behind the desk to turn on the tape recorder.*)

TINA. Sometimes I wonder if I'm made for marriage.

ANDY. Well, your basic equipment is right.

TINA. (*Hears recorder go on.*) What's that?

ANDY. The air conditioning. (*He makes* TINA *comfortable in chair near desk, lights cigarette for her.*) Tell me about your marital experiences. Might do you good to talk.

TINA. You could be right. I don't even have a girl friend to confide in.

ANDY. You poor, lonely kid. How old were you the first time you walked up the aisle?

TINA. Sixteen. A mature sixteen.

ANDY. That *is* the best kind.

TINA. He was the captain of the football team. We eloped after the last game of the season. (*Shakes her head.*) Those athletes with the big muscles really fool you.

ANDY. I've told girls that for years. Who was your lucky No. 2?

TINA. No. 2? No. 2? Oh, a sailor I met at Fisherman's Wharf. We had our eye on the same lobster. And you know how one thing leads to another.

ANDY. Lobster parties can get pretty wild. I know about your third marriage—the Army sergeant. But why go for Jonathan when you still had the Marine Corps?

TINA. Andy, were you ever poor? Really poor?

ANDY. I was, but my parents were rich.

TINA. Mine weren't. My father couldn't hold a job. He was a charter member of Alcoholics Anonymous, but he was always letting his membership lapse.

ANDY. Where is he now?

TINA. Working in a brewery in Milwaukee. The fumes make him so sick that he can't drink. My mother wrote me she's never been happier.

ANDY. Why do you think you'll be happy if you marry for money?

TINA. Why not? I've tried love. All my life I've fallen for schnooks. Not that I'm promiscuous, Andy. I never went to bed with anyone I didn't like.

ANDY. Good girl.

TINA. Then I met Johnny. He was everything I wanted my father to be. And he wooed me. Johnny was the first man in my life who ever wooed me.

ANDY. Have you told him about your three husbands —and the other poor but passionate schnooks in your life?

TINA. Of course not. He's not that broadminded.

ANDY. What do you suppose would happen if someone else told him?

TINA. Who's going to? You? Not unless you want to be disbarred. (*Crosses behind desk.*) That's why I didn't care when you turned on the air conditioning.

ANDY. What air conditioning?

TINA. The one that recorded everything we said. (*Picks up mike, speaks into it.*) Johnny's mine and I'm his. No one's going to stop me from the dream of my life. This is the future Mrs. Jonathan Bentley now signing off. (*Turns off tape.*) Do you suppose Dr. X would take me to lunch?

ANDY. I'll ask him. (*Crosses to his office, calls off.*) Oh, Dr. X—I mean Dr. Fenwick—would you like to take a beautiful young lady to lunch?

DR. FENWICK. (*Enters in doorway.*) If Amelia doesn't mind. We were squeezing in an extra thirty minutes on the couch. (AMELIA *enters in doorway, straightening her hair.*)

AMELIA. I was just going good.

DR. FENWICK. Try to remember where we left off.

TINA. (*Shocked.*) It's none of my business, but this is no way to run a law office.

AMELIA. I don't follow you.

DR. FENWICK. Neither do I. (*Tics violently.*)

TINA. (*To* ANDY.) Does he always shake his head "yes" when he means "no"?

ANDY. Maybe you can find out at lunch. In the meantime, I'll phone West Germany to see what's holding up your annulment papers.

TINA. (*To* DR. FENWICK.) Meet you outside, Doctor.

Maybe we can find out what I'm really like. I'm dying to know.

DR. FENWICK. (*Tic-ing.*) So am I.

TINA. (*To* ANDY.) Sorry about the air-conditioning. (*She exits.*)

DR. FENWICK. Why is she having lunch with me? I'm not her type.

ANDY. She thinks you're Amelia's Mr. X.

AMELIA. Andy, you're brilliant!

ANDY. I'll settle for a raise or my name on the door.

DR. FENWICK. (*To* AMELIA.) I'm Mr. X—the one who wrote those letters? The one with the over-active glands?

AMELIA. Now you can make your doodles come true.

DR. FENWICK. (*Concerned.*) Say, maybe she'll expect me to live up to his reputation.

AMELIA. Tina's too smart. She'll be Miss Faithful until she's Mrs. Bentley.

ANDY. (*Enigmatically.*) I wouldn't count on it. (*Escorts* DR. FENWICK *to door.*) Have a good lunch and don't fight your basic instincts.

DR. FENWICK. Thank you, Doctor. (*He tics strongly, exits.*)

ANDY. He's sick. (*Crosses to* AMELIA.) Now break into your biggest smile.

AMELIA. Give me a good reason.

ANDY. I've got enough on Tina to make Jonathan throw her over.

AMELIA. (*Smiling.*) That's a good reason.

ANDY. I've got enough on her to make him come crawling back.

AMELIA. Who wants him in that position?

ANDY. (*Points.*) She talked her head off on the tape recorder. She talked and it recorded. Do you know why she's marrying Jonathan?

AMELIA. Because he's great on skis.

ANDY. No, she's in love with his money. She's in

love with everything her first three husbands couldn't give her.

AMELIA. Three like in one-two-three?

ANDY. But she never slept with anyone she didn't like. (*Points.*) It's all on that tape. Beautiful?

AMELIA. (*Elated.*) Andy, you're a genius!

ANDY. Who's arguing?

AMELIA. Your name goes on the door tomorrow. Play it for me. Loud and clear. Then guard it with your life. (*Tardy realization.*) What am I saying? We can't use that tape. She's my client.

ANDY. Drop the case.

AMELIA. Unethical. (*Unhappily.*) Destroy it, Andy. Erase the tape.

ANDY. And my name on the door?

AMELIA. (*Pacing.*) If there was only one loophole in our damned code of ethics.

ANDY. May I make a suggestion?

AMELIA. No, Andy, we mustn't be tempted. We cannot play that tape for Jonathan. We can't even tell him it exists.

ANDY. We won't. But suppose he hears it accidentally?

AMELIA. (*Firmly.*) No. Absolutely no. (*After a beat.*) How accidentally? How unethically?

ANDY. Borderline.

AMELIA. No, why should I save him from her? They deserve each other.

ANDY. But you love him. That justifies anything.

AMELIA. (*Stares at tape recorder.*) Well, just don't stand there.

ANDY. I knew your keen analytical mind would prevail. (*Lowers inter-com key.*) Julie, could you stop reading Playboy and come in here? (*To AMELIA.*) What size did you have in mind for my name on the door? (JULIE *enters in doorway.*) Please get Tina's bridegroom-to-be on the phone.

AMELIA. Then try to reach her husband in West Germany.

JULIE. Right away. Say, you should have seen the way Tina looked at Dr. Fenwick when they left. He was tic-ing in all directions. (*Twitches in imitation.*)

AMELIA. Let's hope they reach the moon together.

JULIE. Is there any special reason for throwing Tina and Dr. Fenwick together?

AMELIA. A purely patriotic reason.

ANDY. Patriotic?

AMELIA. With his twitch and her sex drive, they could solve the energy crisis. (JULIE *smiles and exits.*) What are you going to say to Jonathan?

ANDY. Oh, you're going to talk to him. You're going to tell him you're sorry about everything you've done.

AMELIA. But I'm not.

ANDY. You're going to tell him you want to turn his bank accounts back to him. And the stocks and bonds. That should bring him flying.

AMELIA. Without a plane. What happens when he gets here?

ANDY. I take over. Or don't you want him back?

AMELIA. I want him.

ANDY. Okay, then I'll put the tape recorder out of order.

AMELIA. Out of order?

ANDY. Jonathan can fix it when he gets here. Didn't you always tell me he was mechanical-minded?

AMELIA. You should see him with an electric can opener.

ANDY. I'll describe the scene. When he arrives, Julie brings him into the office.

AMELIA. Where are *we?*

ANDY. Hiding in the library. On the desk Jonathan sees a tape recorder. A *broken* tape recorder.

AMELIA. But it's not broken beyond repair?

ANDY. Oh, no! Nothing that a handy man couldn't

fix with a handy screwdriver. What else do you think is on the desk? Right next to the tape recorder?

AMELIA. Tell me, Counsellor.

ANDY. A roll of tape. A roll of tape marked "Tina Salisbury—secret and confidential." Now what would you do in Jonathan's place? Sit there and wait for you? Or try to fix the machine and play the tape?

AMELIA. I'm not sure, but I know what I'm going to do right now.

ANDY. What?

AMELIA. Go paint your name on the door. (*She exits.* ANDY *grins after her.*)

### BLACKOUT—*CURTAIN*

### *END OF ACT ONE*

# ACT TWO

## SCENE 1

SCENE: *The same.*

AT RISE: *It is six p.m. the same day. A tape recorder, partially dismantled, sits on desk. Beside it is a cassette in a box. It bears over-sized handwriting that identifies its contents. The door opens and* JULIE *enters, followed by* JONATHAN.

JONATHAN. (*Annoyed.*) What do you mean she's not here? We had a definite appointment.

JULIE. I know, Mr. Bentley.

JONATHAN. (*Caustically.*) Where *is* the eminent Miss Conway?

JULIE. She went out with Andy to take a deposition. They expected to be back by five.

JONATHAN. (*Looks at watch.*) It's six o'clock now. (*Petulantly.*) Nobody's anywhere.

JULIE. I'm here.

JONATHAN. Tina isn't in, either. She hasn't been at her hotel since this morning.

JULIE. She had a doctor's appointment when she left here. And she phoned around two-thirty that she'd be back before the office closed.

JONATHAN. Doctor? What doctor? She never mentioned any doctor to me.

JULIE. (*With innuendo.*) Might be a lot of things she never mentioned to you.

JONATHAN. What's that supposed to mean?

JULIE. We're her attorneys. You know, confidential relationship between client and—

JONATHAN. (*Interrupts.*) You're a secretary, not an

attorney. What did Tina say that I'm not supposed to know?

JULIE. I didn't say she had. Why don't you have a drink while you're waiting? (*She opens bar.*)

JONATHAN. I don't like to drink alone.

JULIE. Thanks, but I have a date with a San Francisco '49-er and I'm going to need all my strength. (*Goes behind bar, holds up bottles.*) Scotch? Bourbon? Vodka?

JONATHAN. I'll pour it myself, thanks. (*Crosses to bar, fixes drink. JULIE looks at desk.*)

JULIE. Oh, dear!

JONATHAN. You talking to me?

JULIE. The repairman. He never showed up to fix the tape recorder.

JONATHAN. What's wrong with it?

JULIE. The sound. Andy tried to adjust it, but It only got worse.

JONATHAN. Lawyers shouldn't try to be engineers. (*Crosses to desk with drink.*) I could probably fix it in two minutes.

JULIE. Why don't you? It'll keep you busy until your wife gets back.

JONATHAN. No, thanks. I go on overtime after six. She couldn't afford me.

JULIE. That's too bad. We really do need it first thing in the morning. (*Crosses to door.*) Would you mind if I left? I don't want to be late for my date. (*JONATHAN sips drink, glances at box of tape. He reads the printing on it, nearly chokes.*) Are you all right, Mr. Bentley?

JONATHAN. (*Stares at tape.*) I will be as soon as you leave. (*Over-casually.*) You wouldn't have a screw driver, would you?

JULIE. There's one in the top drawer. Andy put it there especially. I mean, it's the one he was using.

JONATHAN. Thanks. I'll have it fixed before Amelia gets back.

JULIE. We all hope so. Well, I'm off to an evening of intercepted passes. (*She exits.* JONATHAN *opens drawer, takes out screw driver, then picks up tape.*)

JONATHAN. Tina baby, this is none of my business, but I damn well want to hear it! (*As he works, sings.*) I'm a rambling wreck from Georgia Tech—and a helluva engineer. (*Cocks head to read writing on box.*) "Tina Salisbury—secret and confidential." Well, not for long. A wife shouldn't keep any secrets from her husband. (*Tests machine.*) Call in the engineers, I always say. (*He puts on cassette, runs it back, sets control at proper speed, turns recorder on.*)

TINA'S VOICE. What's that?

ANDY'S VOICE. The air conditioning. Tell me all about your marital experiences. It'll do you good to talk.

TINA'S VOICE. You might be right. I don't even have a girl friend to confide in.

JONATHAN. You've got *me*.

ANDY'S VOICE. How old were you the first time you got married?

(MRS. HORTON *enters. She has obviously had a few drinks.* JONATHAN *dives for the "stop" button. The next words on the tape trail off.*)

MRS. HORTON. Hello there! Am I interrupting something?

JONATHAN. Not a thing. I just repaired the tape recorder and I wanted to see if it worked.

MRS. HORTON. Does it?

JONATHAN. You came in before I could make sure.

MRS. HORTON. Well, you go right ahead, Mr. Bentley. (*Crosses to bar unsteadily.*) I've been drinking, or can't you tell?

JONATHAN. (*Eyes tape recorder.*) Do you plan to stay for awhile?

MRS. HORTON. Until Amelia gets back. I just met

Julie at the elevator and she told me to wait in the outer office. But you know how I am.

JONATHAN. As a matter of fact, I don't.

MRS. HORTON. I mean I'm always coming in here unannounced. (*She raises her foot to put it on a non-existent bar rail, misses, almost falls.*)

JONATHAN. Amelia just phoned. She won't be back for at least an hour. You don't want to hang around here doing nothing.

MRS. HORTON. Oh, I won't be doing nothing. I'll be drinking. (*Pours liquor into glass.*) I do have to see Amelia. There's been a new development in my divorce case.

JONATHAN. (*Looks at tape.*) Mine, too. Mrs. Horton, how would you like to go to the bar on the ground floor and get smashed at my expense?

MRS. HORTON. (*Understandingly.*) It's the children. You don't want to talk about it because you're sensitive about the children. How are they taking it?

JONATHAN. We have no children.

MRS. HORTON. Why not?

JONATHAN. After six years we gave up. We thought maybe if we didn't try so hard, it might just happen.

MRS. HORTON. (*Sympathetically.*) But it never did.

JONATHAN. I would have liked a son. Someone to follow in my footsteps. Carry on my name. Amelia felt the same way.

MRS. HORTON. (*Bewildered.*) Amelia? What's her relation to the children you didn't have?

JONATHAN. (*Patiently.*) Amelia is my wife. This is my wife's office. She's handling my next wife's annulment.

MRS. HORTON. Mr. Bentley, you've been drinking.

JONATHAN. (*Crosses to bar.*) Not enough. (*Irritably.*) I left word for Tina to call me here. Why hasn't she?

MRS. HORTON. Tina is your Rosalie? (JONATHAN *eyes her questioningly, freshens his drink.*) She's the new secretary I hired for my husband—the girl I just caught Oliver with. That's my husband. And where do you think I caught them? In the motel he bought me when I called off the divorce. They didn't even wait for the Christmas office party.

JONATHAN. Some people like to do their shopping early. I don't want to be nosy, but what were you doing at the motel in the afternoon?

MRS. HORTON. After we finished playing backgammon, the girls wanted to sober up before they went home. So we drove by my motel to see how business was. The place was jammed with cars.

JONATHAN. It would be around five. Tourists who want a good night's rest before they drive on to Los Angeles.

MRS. HORTON. Right in the middle of all those cars was Oliver's Mercedes Benz. He was a fool to buy a flaming red one.

JONATHAN. Fool? He was out of his mind!

MRS. HORTON. I got out and told the other girls to go on. That I had to check on something.

JONATHAN. Someone has to be the foreman.

MRS. HORTON. I was most discreet. I just sat in Oliver's car and waited until he came out with Rosalie.

JONATHAN. What did the brazen hussy do?

MRS. HORTON. She just looked at Oliver and said, "I've never been so disappointed in my life," and drove off in her car. I have a feeling Oliver's going to fire her tomorrow.

JONATHAN. Then what happened?

MRS. HORTON. Oliver must have been in an awful hurry when he got there because he'd left the keys in his car.

JONATHAN. It's happened to all of us.

MRS. HORTON. So I drove off with him running alongside yelling, "It's all in your mind! I hardly know the girl!"

JONATHAN. He does sound sincere.

MRS. HORTON. (*Rises from couch, her legs wobbling.*) Are we having an earthquake?

JONATHAN. Not over here.

MRS. HORTON. Well, I came right over—except for a stop at the bar downstairs. To give me enough backbone to go through with the divorce this time. (*Begins to cry drunken tears.*) How can a man be so physical after a hard day's work at the office?

JONATHAN. You'll dilute your drink with those tears.

MRS. HORTON. Oh, don't worry about me. I'm not too old to find someone else. Like Amelia is.

JONATHAN. (*Defensively.*) Amelia is not too old. She's in the prime of life. She's a fine woman who doesn't deserve what I'm doing to her.

MRS. HORTON. Then why are you doing it?

JONATHAN. Damned if I know. But I've been doing it all my life.

MRS. HORTON. There never should have been two sexes. Then this kind of thing wouldn't happen.

JONATHAN. That's a wonderful exit line, Mrs. Horton. I really must work on the tape recorder.

MRS. HORTON. And I want you to. I'll just pour myself one more little one— (*She fills her glass full. JONATHAN crosses to desk.*) then I'll sit and watch you. (*She crosses to chair near desk, waits for JONATHAN to start recorder.*)

JONATHAN. (*Patience cracking.*) Mrs. Horton, I have to play this tape before Amelia gets back.

MRS. HORTON. Well, I certainly have no objection.

JONATHAN. *Alone.*

MRS. HORTON. (*Waggishly.*) Why? Aren't you supposed to hear it?

JONATHAN. I am, but you're not.

MRS. HORTON. I'm not budging. I want to hear it, too.

JONATHAN. Okay then, hear it. (*He pushes high speed lever, plays tape. The voices are high-pitched gibberish.*) See? It doesn't work right. (*Turns off tape, crosses to bar.*) How about joining me at the bar?

MRS. HORTON. Don't you want to hear the tape?

JONATHAN. I'll take it with me and play it at home. (*His back is to* MRS. HORTON *as he looks under bar for fresh bottle. She pushes re-run button on recorder and another lever.* JONATHAN *turns, startled.*) What are you doing?

MRS. HORTON. You were running it at the wrong speed. Now try it.

JONATHAN. (*Hurries to desk, stops the tape recorder frantically. Hoarsely.*) Do you know what you've done?

MRS. HORTON. Run the tape back. I know how to work it. We have one at home.

JONATHAN. Do you know what you did when you ran it back? You erased it! Where the hell have you been working—the White House?

MRS. HORTON. Oh, dear! That's the one thing I always do wrong. It makes Oliver furious.

JONATHAN. Mrs. Horton, Oliver deserves a hundred Rosalies. No, a thousand! You've ruined my life by not letting me find out about Tina's.

MRS. HORTON. Don't you trust the girl you're going to marry?

JONATHAN. Of course I trust her. I just want to know what the hell she's hiding from me.

MRS. HORTON. Say, maybe I didn't erase everything. Play it and see. (JONATHAN *starts tape. It plays silently for long stretch.*) They're very quiet, aren't they?

TINA'S VOICE. (*From tape recorder.*) This is the future-Mrs. Jonathan Bentley, now signing off.

MRS. HORTON. Doesn't sound like she said anything incriminating ahead of that.

JONATHAN. I'm not sure. I want to hear her reading again. (*He runs tape back, starts recorder.*)

TINA'S VOICE. This is the future Mrs. Jonathan Bentley, now signing off.

AMELIA. (*Followed by* ANDY, *enters. They're in time to hear the last line.*) *Aha!*

JONATHAN. Aha what?

ANDY. (*Points accusingly.*) That was a private conversation, Mr. Bentley. You had no right to listen to it.

AMELIA. Why, Johnny wouldn't do a thing like that. Would you, Johnny?

JONATHAN. Who are you calling Johnny?

ANDY. That was the last line on the tape. He must have heard the whole thing.

MRS. HORTON. (*Brightly.*) Oh, no, he didn't. What happened was—

JONATHAN. (*Interrupting.*) Shut up, Mrs. Horton. (*To* AMELIA.) All your clients talk too much. Tina shot her mouth off on tape— (*Points at* MRS. HORTON.) and she just told me about her husband's adventures in a motel.

AMELIA. With his own wife? What's wrong with that?

JONATHAN. Someone else played her part today.

AMELIA. (*To* MRS. HORTON.) Anyone we know?

MRS. HORTON. Rosalie. I hired her myself. And her references were excellent. Her mother said she was a wonderful girl.

AMELIA. You should have checked her mother's references. Andy, drive Mrs. Horton home in her car and come back in a cab.

ANDY. Can't she take a cab and pick up her car tomorrow? I'd like to be in on the kill.

AMELIA. (*Firmly.*) Goodbye, Andy.

ANDY. (*Sighs, takes* MRS. HORTON *by the arm.*) It looks like we're not wanted. (*Crossing to door.*) Where are you parked?

MRS. HORTON. Right in front. Between the fire hydrant and the no-parking sign.

ANDY. That shouldn't be hard to find. (*He exits with her.*)

JONATHAN. Not that I care, but doesn't Mrs. Horton have a first name?

AMELIA. Smirnoff. Aren't you ashamed—listening to that tape?

JONATHAN. Ashamed? I ought to send you a bill for repairs.

AMELIA. (*Reaching for recorder.*) How does the machine work now?

JONATHAN. Fine, just fine.

AMELIA. Then you did hear the tape?

JONATHAN. Every word on it.

AMELIA. And you see a future with a girl with that much of a past?

JONATHAN. Exactly what are you referring to on that tape?

AMELIA. I can't discuss it with you. It's confidential.

JONATHAN. But I can discuss it with you?

AMELIA. Technically, yes.

JONATHAN. (*Casually.*) What's confidential about— (*Probing.*) the other men in Tina's life?

AMELIA. I can't say.

JONATHAN. Has Tina been married more than once?

AMELIA. I can't say.

JONATHAN. Has she been divorced more than once?

AMELIA. I can't say.

JONATHAN. Have there been other men in her life?

AMELIA. I can't say.

JONATHAN. (*Exasperated.*) All right, then, who's the doctor she was going to see this afternoon?

AMELIA. That I can say. She went to lunch with him.

JONATHAN. What for?

AMELIA. I guess she was hungry.

JONATHAN. Amelia, I know that look in your eye. You're hiding something.

AMELIA. Why get upset just because she had lunch with another man?

JONATHAN. Because she isn't back at her hotel yet. That's why. It doesn't take a doctor six hours to take her pulse.

AMELIA. He's not that kind of a doctor. He's an analyst.

JONATHAN. There's nothing to analyze about Tina. She's what she is. A sweet, decent girl who didn't know much about life until she met me.

AMELIA. You must have played that tape awfully fast.

JONATHAN. (*Indicates recorder.*) She'll be glad to repeat everything she told Andy.

AMELIA. If she ever gets back to the hotel.

JONATHAN. What's that doctor's name? (*Crosses to desk.*) Maybe he'll know where she went.

AMELIA. Have another drink and I'll play secretary for you, darling. (*Gets phone book.*)

JONATHAN. Amelia, don't pick on me. I'm tired. I had a hard week in the mountains.

AMELIA. Maybe you're getting too old to handle a job and a young wife at the same time. (*Finds number.*) It's Dr. Fenwick's day off. His service'll probably answer.

JONATHAN. Just find him and ask him where I can find Tina.

AMELIA. (*Dialing.*) They did seem to like each other. Does that bother you?

JONATHAN. Is Fenwick the one I met here a couple weeks ago? (*Tics.*) The twitcher?

AMELIA. He has a wonderful couch-side manner. (*Into phone.*) Oh, hello, Dr. Fenwick. What are you doing in your office? (*Listens, smiles happily.*) Really? . . . All afternoon? . . . Where is she now? . . . Thanks a lot. (*Hangs up.*)

JONATHAN. I don't believe a word you're going to say.

AMELIA. I'll say it anyway. They had lunch—Tina and Dr. Fenwick—and then she told him she felt like talking. About herself. So they went to his office.

JONATHAN. Why couldn't they talk at lunch?

AMELIA. Dr. Fenwick has a hangup about listening to women while they're lying on a couch. He says Tina's all mixed up, but he's going to straighten her out.

JONATHAN. You tell him to keep his hands to himself,

AMELIA. He's an analyst, not a chiropractor.

JONATHAN. He's a man, too, and Tina has a strange way of affecting men.

AMELIA. (*Looks at tape recorder.*) I know.

JONATHAN. Where is she now?

AMELIA. On her way here, and don't worry. Psychiatrists never play around with their patients.

JONATHAN. Ha! I wish I had a dollar for every analyst who locked the door, faced his diploma to the wall, and turned up the Muzac in his office.

AMELIA. If you really feel that way, ask Tina what went on today. I bet she won't even admit she spent the afternoon with the doctor. Or that she has reservations about you.

JONATHAN. (*Raises voice.*) Who said she talked about me? Who's even sure they talked?

AMELIA. (*Crosses to bar.*) You're shouting.

JONATHAN. Who's shouting?

AMELIA. And when you shout you're suspicious. And when you're suspicious, you're usually right.

JONATHAN. (*Follows her.*) Don't try to flatter me with the truth, Amelia.

AMELIA. (*Fixes drinks.*) About that tape recording. Ask Tina to play it for you. Or don't you dare?

JONATHAN. What if she will?

AMELIA. She won't.

JONATHAN. What if she will? What if she'll let me hear whatever you talked her into saying?

AMELIA. Then I'll quit. I'll quit putting up a fight for you.

JONATHAN. I'll drink to that. (*AMELIA hands him drink. They click glasses.*)

AMELIA. To fifteen miserably wonderful years.

JONATHAN. (*Takes taste.*) Nobody can pour a drink like you do.

AMELIA. Call me whenever you have a party. I'll stay in the kitchen and nobody'll even know I'm there. (*Phone rings.*)

JONATHAN. If that's Tina, I want to talk to her.

AMELIA. (*Crosses to phone.*) She probably wants to report she stopped at the hotel to change. Clothes can get awfully creased—all those hours on the couch. (*Into phone.*) Hello . . . Yes, we're ready to take the call. (*Hand over mouthpiece.*) It's Tina's husband. Do you want to talk to *him?*

JONATHAN. I thought he was in Germany.

AMELIA. He is.

JONATHAN. What the hell does he want?

AMELIA. *We* called *him.* (*Into phone.*) Hello, Sergeant Harrington. This is Amelia Conway, your wife's attorney . . . your wife Tina. The one you married because you thought you were going to be a father.

JONATHAN. Amelia, that's no way to maintain Army morale.

AMELIA. (*Continued.*) Now you remember her? Good. I'm calling about the papers we sent you—the annulment papers . . . Yes, she wants to get married again . . . No, I don't know who the stupid jerk is.

JONATHAN. (*Grabs phone angrily. Into phone.*) Well, I know who the stupid jerk is. I'm the stupid jerk! Who the hell do you think you are talking about me like that? I happen to be one of the taxpayers who's giving you an all-expense vacation in Europe!

AMELIA. Be nice, Johnny, or he won't sign anything.

JONATHAN. Oh . . . (*Into phone.*) Who the hell said "who the hell"? We must have a bad connection

. . . Hold the line a minute. (*Hand over mouthpiece.*) He says if I marry Tina, he'll bet it won't last.

AMELIA. You heard the tape.

JONATHAN. As far as I'm concerned, there's nothing on it. (*Into phone.*) It's been nice talking with you, Captain. Keep an eye out for Dr. Kissinger and those Russians. (*Hands phone to* AMELIA.)

AMELIA. Hello again. How do you like Tina's next husband? . . . No, he just sounds old over long distance. What *is* the status of the annulment papers? . . . Thank you, Sergeant. (*Hangs up.*) He airmailed everything yesterday. You and Tina can plan to go on your honeymoon in a couple of weeks.

JONATHAN. Thanks, Amelia.

AMELIA. Unless Dr. Fenwick talked her out of marrying you.

JONATHAN. I wouldn't count on it.

AMELIA. Or if you change your mind after Tina refuses to play that tape.

JONATHAN. I wouldn't count on that, either.

AMELIA. All right, I won't. But remember this. Two months or two years from now—when Tina finds out you can pay the bills but it's more fun to go skiing with the ski instructor—don't come limping back to me with your broken heart in a cast.

JONATHAN. No chance. It's too late, Amelia.

AMELIA. It's never too late. You're old enough to grow up.

JONATHAN. Will you stop being Miss Conway most of the time and be Mrs. Bentley all the time?

AMELIA. How can I? I've got an office full of clients —cases in court and out-of-court. I can't just pull up and—

JONATHAN. (*Interrupts.*) Forget it! You stick with your career and I'll stick with Tina. And do you know why? Because nothing means anything to her except me. That sounds pretty good to a man my age. (*Outer office door opens offstage.*)

AMELIA. That must be Tina baby. (*The door opens and* TINA *enters.*)

TINA. (*Surprised.*) Johnny! What are you doing here?

JONATHAN. (*Crosses to embrace her.*) I was lonesome for you. Were you lonesome for me?

AMELIA. Of course she was. That's why her lipstick is smeared.

TINA. Is it? (*Looks in mirror.*) It is not! (*Kisses* JONATHAN *warmly.*) Now it's smeared.

AMELIA. That is the guiltiest kiss I ever saw.

JONATHAN. Really? (*To* TINA.) Darling, where were you all afternoon?

TINA. With Dr. Fenwick. He's an analyst and the most wonderful listener. It's the first time I ever *talked* on a couch for three hours.

JONATHAN. (*Triumphantly, to* AMELIA.) Well?

AMELIA. I've been wrong before.

TINA. Johnny, I've changed my mind about the engagement ring and the mink coat and my own Jaguar. All I want you to give me is one teeny-weeny present.

AMELIA. The Bank of America?

JONATHAN. Name it and it's yours.

TINA. I want you to give me Dr. Fenwick.

JONATHAN. Could you word that a little differently?

TINA. I want to see him five days a week until we get married.

JONATHAN. You what?

AMELIA. Oh, she'll find time to squeeze you in somewhere.

TINA. It's important to me, Johnny. I just discovered that I've got complexes.

JONATHAN. (*Boils over.*) Complexes? You did this, Amelia Conway Bentley! You threw her together with that four-eyed Fenwick. Tina never had an inhibited bone in her body.

AMELIA. It wasn't my idea for her to get chummy

with the good doctor. She invited him to lunch herself. He just tic-ed and she tic-ed back.

JONATHAN. (*Accusing, to* TINA.) Did you?

TINA. I only had lunch with him to get evidence for you. He's her Mr. X. (JONATHAN *glares at* AMELIA.)

JONATHAN. (*To* AMELIA, *astounded.*) Twitchy?!

AMELIA. No comment.

JONATHAN. So that's the sonofabitch who grew horns on me! (*Turns on* TINA.) And you want to spend five days a week with him? A man who doesn't respect a woman's wedding ring!

AMELIA. You didn't respect yours.

JONATHAN. I never played around with a married woman in all my life.

AMELIA. That's a pretty fine line of demarcation.

TINA. What does "demarcation" mean?

AMELIA. Take a dictionary on your honeymoon. It'll give you something to do on your second night. (*Tosses tape box to her.*) Here's something else for you to read.

TINA. There's nothing secret or confidential in my life. Ask Dr. Fenwick. I told him everything.

AMELIA. In one afternoon?

JONATHAN. You told him, but have you told me?

TINA. It's a trick, Johnny, a trick to break us up. Look—the box is empty.

AMELIA. The tape that was in that box is on this tape recorder.

TINA. All right, then, play it.

AMELIA. You know I can't.

TINA. (*To* JONATHAN.) Are you going to believe me or do you want to hear it?

JONATHAN. I want to believe you, Tina.

AMELIA. But he'd rather hear the tape. Why don't you play it, Tina? I'll show you how to run the machine. All it can cost you is one husband.

TINA. All right, I'll play it. Jonathan loves me

enough not to let anything make a difference. (*Crosses to recorder.*) How do you start this damn thing?

AMELIA. (*Suits action to words.*) First, we rewind the tape. Like so. Now you press this little button— the one that says "It was nice knowing you, Johnny" —and turn up the sound so we can hear it loud and clear.

TINA. Dr. Fenwick says there's nothing in my life to be ashamed of. (*She reaches for tape recorder. JONATHAN catches her arm.*)

JONATHAN. You were wrong again, Amelia.

ANDY. (*Enters, completely dejected.*) Thank God the bar's still open. (*Crosses to pour drink.*) I may kill myself. *And* Mrs. Horton.

AMELIA. You're just in time. Tina's going to play my favorite recording.

ANDY. Don't strain your ears. There's nothing on the tape. Mrs. Horton told me how she accidentally erased it.

TINA. (*Relieved.*) There's nothing on the tape?

JONATHAN. Nothing much. (*To AMELIA.*) Tina didn't know that, but she was willing to let me hear it.

TINA. (*Regaining confidence.*) Why not? I didn't have anything to hide.

AMELIA. I don't believe it. (*She runs tape back, then forward.*)

TINA'S VOICE. (*On tape.*) This is the future Mrs. Jonathan Bentley, now signing off. (AMELIA *stops tape recorder.*)

AMELIA. I could kill the man who invented the eraser.

TINA. (*Takes JONATHAN'S arm.*) Shall we go, Johnny?

JONATHAN. Just a minute. (*Crosses to AMELIA.*) I'm sorry to do this to you, Amelia.

AMELIA. I've lost cases before. Maybe not as important, but I have lost.

ANDY. (*Consoling.*) You still have Mr. X.

AMELIA. Goodbye, Jonathan. I'll let you know when you and Tina can make it legal. In the meantime, enjoy yourselves.

TINA. How can we? With Johnny up in the mountains and me down here with Dr. Fenwick?

JONATHAN. (*Firmly.*) You'll be down here, but not with that psychiatric lecher.

AMELIA. Don't be so selfish, Johnny. The girl needs help.

JONATHAN. Not from Dr. Fenwick, she doesn't.

AMELIA. Jonathan, let her see Dr. Fenwick and I'll release your bank accounts and the stocks and bonds.

TINA. What bank accounts? What stocks and bonds?

JONATHAN. Don't bother your pretty little head with business details. (*To* AMELIA.) Okay, it's a deal. Blackmailer! (*He exits with* TINA. AMELIA *looks after them, emotionally exhausted.* ANDY *crosses to her with drinks.*)

AMELIA. Andy, how do I look?

ANDY. Drip-dried. Now what?

AMELIA. (*Toasting each other.*) It all depends on Dr. Fenwick's couch.

### *CURTAIN*

### ACT TWO

#### SCENE 2

SCENE: *The same.*

AT RISE: *It is an afternoon three weeks later.* ANDY *is packing law books into a cardboard carton. Several other cartons are already full. Two pieces of airline luggage stand near* AMELIA's *desk.* JULIE *arranges flowers in a vase on the desk.*

ANDY. I've lived in San Francisco all my life. Outside of six years at Harvard. How am I going to like Los Angeles?

JULIE. You don't have to go with Amelia. As a matter of fact, I don't know why she has to go.

ANDY. Southern California can use someone like Amelia.

JULIE. She needs a new man in her life, not a change of venue. (*Phone rings.* JULIE *answers.*) Miss Conway's office . . . No, she isn't back from court yet, Mr. Bentley. Miss Salisbury's getting her annulment today . . . I know you know . . . I imagine she went to her hotel . . . Oh, you just went up to her room and she wasn't there? Maybe she went to Dr. Fenwick's. (*Reacts as* JONATHAN *hangs up sharply.*) He's looking for his blushing bride-to-be. (*Hangs up.*)

ANDY. It must be thirty minutes since Amelia called and said Tina was a free woman.

JULIE. Miss Conway's still in love with her husband, isn't she?

ANDY. Always will be, I guess. The other day she confessed to me that Jonathan was the only man she'd ever slept with.

JULIE. It's hard to believe in this day and age.

ANDY. Her generation has some weird hangups. Why, when I was at Harvard, two seniors at Wellesley were virgins. The other girls said they were trying to give the school a bad name.

JULIE. I went to Stanford. A girl really gets an education there.

ANDY. It rates high scholastically, too.

JULIE. (*Looks around.*) I'm going to miss this office. I'll even miss you, Andy. I was becoming quite fond of you.

ANDY. Were you really? (*She nods.*) I wish I could tell Dr. Fenwick.

JULIE. Why can't you?

ANDY. After I get settled in Los Angeles, I'll tell

my new analyst. He'll probably agree it's important I
get away from you.

JULIE. Away from me?

ANDY. I finally got rid of my mother. Psychiatrically
speaking, that is. Now I have to eliminate you.

JULIE. Andy, all we've ever been are friendly co-
workers. You've never even kissed me.

ANDY. Don't rub it in.

JULIE. What kind of doctor is Fenwick, anyway?
Why should he try to break up an affair that never
existed?

ANDY. I lied to him.

JULIE. At the prices you pay?

ANDY. I couldn't admit the girl I'm crazy about
won't even go out with me. He thinks we've been
having a ball.

JULIE. Andy, if I didn't like you so much—

ANDY. Do you really?

JULIE. Of course I do, but I can't see myself taking
you home to meet my father. He's six-foot-six.

ANDY. I could sit in the car. Then he wouldn't know
how tall I am.

JULIE. It won't work. But don't give up. You still
might catch me on the rebound from one of the basket-
ball players I date.

ANDY. Shall we drink to that?

JULIE. This is hardly a day to celebrate. (*Indicates
flowers.*) Amelia's birthday—and she spent most of it
in court with Tina. Why weren't you there?

ANDY. I'm not an attorney—I'm a moving man.
Amelia wants out of this town as soon as possible.
Tina's her last case here—the candle on the cake.

JULIE. When is the wedding?

ANDY. In Reno tomorrow. After Johnny baby gets
his divorce. (*He brings bar into view. It's empty except for several glasses on bar and a bottle on a high
shelf.*)

JULIE. I left one bottle in case Amelia needs a shot.

ANDY. (*Goes behind bar.*) How about having our first drink on our last day together?

JULIE. It's not the end of the world, Andy. L.A. is full of tall girls.

ANDY. And tall men. I'll pour you a short one. (JULIE *crosses to door, opens it.* ANDY *stretches for bottle, can't reach it. He steps on box behind bar, stays on it while he pours drinks.*) We'd better have our drink before Amelia arrives.

JULIE. (*Crosses to bar.*) Good idea. You know her office rules.

ANDY. This office doesn't exist any more. We're out of business. (ANDY, *standing on box, is now taller than* JULIE. *She looks up into his eyes.*)

JULIE. Why, Andy! You have one blue eye and one brown.

ANDY. You never gave me a chance to show you. (*Hopefully.*) Julie, as long as I'm up in your neighborhood, could I kiss you goodbye?

JULIE. I was going to make the same suggestion.

(ANDY *leans across bar, kisses her. They break.* JULIE *stares at him, then leans over and kisses him.*)

ANDY. (*Breathless.*) It's exactly like I told Dr. Fenwick. Only better.

JULIE. If I were only sure the children would be tall.

ANDY. We could start giving them shots the day they're born. (*He puts his arms around her, kisses her.* AMELIA *enters, briefcase in hand, crosses to desk after cursory glance at* ANDY *and* JULIE.)

AMELIA. Don't mind me, Julie. As long as it isn't Andy you're kissing. (*Turns, stares.*) My God, it *is* Andy! When did you grow up?

ANDY. (*He and* JULIE *break from kiss, embarrassed.*) I'm standing on something.

JULIE. We were just saying goodbye, Miss Conway. Only maybe it won't be.

ANDY. (*Steps down, holds up empty J & B box.*) I may carry this with me the rest of our lives.

AMELIA. I'm glad to see two happy people today. Tina was as serious in court as I was. Something was bothering her. (*Sees flowers.*) Well, isn't that nice? Who remembered? (ANDY *and* JULIE *point at each other.*) Thank you, children. (*Takes card, reads it.*) "Happy birthday! Mr. X."

ANDY. There will be one in your life.

AMELIA. I wish I were half as sure.

ANDY. How did it go in court?

JULIE. Do you know where Tina is now? Mr. Bentley phoned and said she wasn't at her hotel.

AMELIA. That's not our problem. The corpus delicti is now hers and she can have him.

ANDY. You're not going to file any more appeals?

AMELIA. (*Shakes head.*) Driving back from court, I tried to recall all the things Jonathan did that I foolishly forgave. It was a pretty long list. I must have been crazy.

ANDY. Crazy in love.

AMELIA. (*Picks up framed photograph on desk.*) He never looked this good. You should have seen the picture before it was retouched. (*Tosses it to* JULIE.) File it in the wastebasket. (JULIE *drops picture in wastebasket near desk.*)

ANDY. I'm glad you're over him.

JULIE. He doesn't deserve you.

ANDY. You're too good for him.

AMELIA. (*Wryly.*) Why don't we stop lying to each other? (*To* JULIE *and* ANDY.) Please phone Mrs. Horton at home. I'll close the bar, and you two check if the library is packed.

ANDY. Sure. (*He follows* JULIE, *who exits. He turns at door.*) You saw her kiss me. I've been compromised, haven't I?

AMELIA. (*Taps liquor box.*) You've got a strong case. (ANDY *exits.* AMELIA *reaches on desk to look at*

JONATHAN'S *picture, realizes it isn't there.*) And I've got a lot of bad habits to break.

MRS. HORTON. (*Enters.*) Amelia! Do you know what Andy and your secretary are doing out there?

AMELIA. I could make a pretty good guess.

MRS. HORTON. They didn't even stop. Just motioned for me to go right in.

AMELIA. It's all right. They fell in love today.

MRS. HORTON. So did I. With my husband Oliver. Thank goodness he broke his head this morning. (*Happily.*) Split it wide open.

AMELIA. I don't follow you.

MRS. HORTON. Well, when I made him move out of the house, he moved into the motel just to annoy me.

AMELIA. The culprit always returns to the scene of the crime.

MRS. HORTON. As he stepped out of the shower this morning, he slipped. Got the loveliest concussion when his head hit the tub.

AMELIA. And it knocked some sense into him?

MRS. HORTON. He was delirious for hours. I've been sitting by his bed all day, holding his hand, just listening.

AMELIA. Florence Nightingade.

MRS. HORTON. All he talked about was me. How wonderful I was—how understanding—how desirable.

AMELIA. He *was* delirious.

MRS. HORTON. You can't divorce a man who loves you even when he doesn't know what he's saying. Isn't it a beautiful day, Amelia?

AMELIA. Beautiful. You've got Oliver to nurse back to health, Julie discovered there's more to Andy than meets the eye, and Tina was separated from the Army. (*Indicates flowers.*) And it all happened on my birthday.

MRS. HORTON. Happy birthday, Amelia.

AMELIA. Yes, isn't it? (*Outer office door opens off-stage.*)

ANDY'S VOICE. (*Concerned.*) Mr. Bentley! What happened?

JULIE'S VOICE. Are you all right?

JONATHAN'S VOICE. All right? I'm lucky to be alive! (AMELIA *hurries across room as* JONATHAN *enters.* ANDY *and* JULIE *watch from doorway.* JONATHAN'S *head is completely bandaged, his hand is taped, his arm is in a sling, he wears a taped cast on one foot. Under his other arm is a box of flowers. To* AMELIA.) Don't ask any questions I don't want to answer.

AMELIA. You fell off the ski lift?

MRS. HORTON. The shower! Ask him if he took a shower this morning.

JONATHAN. Mrs. Horton, I would like to be alone with my wife.

AMELIA. (*Crosses, takes him to couch.*) Sit over here, dear. You don't seem to be in any condition for a honeymoon.

JONATHAN. (*Groans as he sits.*) I've aged ten years in the last two hours. (*Stares at others.*) Must we talk in front of hostile witnesses?

AMELIA. Andy, please call the Siegal & O'Brien office for Mrs. Horton. The divorce is off again.

ANDY. Maybe we ought to mimeograph her case and just leave a blank space for changing the date.

MRS. HORTON. (*Crosses to door.*) Goodbye, Amelia, I hope you'll do fine in your new office.

AMELIA. I'll try, but they say there are three young girls in L.A. for every middle-aged man. And each one's trying to get his rightful share.

MRS. HORTON. Well, back to Oliver, the man I love —until I catch him cheating again. (*She exits.*)

JULIE. Come on, big boy.

ANDY. (*Hopefully, to* AMELIA.) You're sure you don't want me to stay? (JULIE'S *arm reaches from offstage and pulls* ANDY *offstage.*)

JONATHAN. What was that about L.A.? (*Looks around.*) Why are you packing everything?

AMELIA. This town has too many memories for me. I can't go West like the pioneers did, so I'm headin' South.

JONATHAN. You'll hate all that sunshine and smog. (*Offers flowers.*) Happy birthday.

AMELIA. I hope you didn't write "I love you, Tina" on the card.

JONATHAN. No, they're for you. (*Sees flowers on desk.*) Who sent you those?

AMELIA. I believe the card is still there. (JONATHAN *rises, limps to desk.*)

JONATHAN. (*Reads card.*) "Happy birthday! Mr. X.?" (*Explodes.*) Twitchy! He dared to send you flowers?

AMELIA. It was only a friendly gesture.

JONATHAN. Gesture? Out! They go out! (*He takes flowers out of vase, dumps them into wastebasket. He sees his framed photograph, picks it up.*) What's my favorite picture doing in the wastebasket? (*Sits it upright on desk.*)

AMELIA. It didn't seem to belong on my desk any more. (JONATHAN *drops the "Mr. X." card into waste-basket.*)

JONATHAN. Neither does he. Amelia, you've made a fool of yourself. He's cheating on you.

AMELIA. How do you know?

JONATHAN. (*Holds up arm in sling.*) That's how I got this. (*Raises leg.*) And sprained my ankle. (*Touches back of head gingerly.*) And cracked my head. That's how I know.

AMELIA. I don't suppose you could start at the beginning?

JONATHAN. If you won't laugh at me.

AMELIA. Have I ever?

JONATHAN. Put my flowers in the vase. It looks empty just sitting there.

AMELIA. (*Opens box.*) Only because you asked so nicely. (*Opens box of flowers.*) Birds of paradise! My favorite. How did you remember with so much on your mind?

JONATHAN. Don't be sarcastic, Amelia. I've had a rough afternoon.

AMELIA. I've had a rough five weeks since the last time you brought me flowers. (*Starts arranging flowers in vase.*)

JONATHAN. Do you want to hear what happened today or do you want to rub salt in my wounds?

AMELIA. Both, frankly.

JONATHAN. As soon as I flew in today, I picked up Tina's wedding present. Then I went to her hotel to pick up Tina. No Tina. The desk clerk gave me a message that she'd be back by four. But I could tell he was holding out on me. You know that desk-clerk smile. Know-all—tell nothing.

AMELIA. They're very close-mouthed.

JONATHAN. I opened his mouth with five dollars. He said Tina rushed in from court and changed into a high-necked dress—then told him she was going to see her doctor and to tell me she'd be back by four.

AMELIA. She probably wanted to ask the doctor what every bride for the fourth time should know.

JONATHAN. She meant Dr. Fenwick. Twitchy! Do you know what day this is?

AMELIA. My birthday.

JONATHAN. Wednesday. Twitchy doesn't play golf and he doesn't keep office hours on Wednesday afternoons, but she went to see him. *Where?*

AMELIA. It's your question.

JONATHAN. I knew what to do—I phoned his office. When he answered, I hung up.

AMELIA. Then you fell down the stairs in your hurry to get there.

JONATHAN. No. I'll tell you something, Amelia. A man should never get sick on a Wednesday afternoon Those medical buildings are like morgues. His outsid door was locked, but I got a cleaning man to open it for me.

AMELIA. There went another five dollars.

JONATHAN. Ten. (*Demonstrates.*) I closed the door and tiptoed across to his consultation room. I could hear voices inside. His and Tina's.

AMELIA. You should have taken along a tape recorder.

JONATHAN. I'll remember every word they said for the rest of my life. "Tina," he said, "tell me how you really feel about your marriage tomorrow." "Awful," she said, "just awful." Heavy breathing.

AMELIA. I hear there's a lot of asthma going around.

JONATHAN. (*Giving her dirty look.*) "Why?" he said. "Because I'm crazy about you," she said. "I want to marry you, not Johnny and his money. He's sweet and he's kind, but he's old enough to be my father." "He's a father image," said Twitchy. Heavy breathing. "So are you, I suppose," she said, "but you'll uncomplex me and I'll be all the better wife for it, won't I, Delbert?" Imagine—his name is Delbert! "Delbert," she said, "please don't fight this. We were meant for each other." Heavy, heavy breathing. "Kiss me," she said, "please kiss me." "Kiss you?" he said. "I shouldn't even be lying here." (*Holds up bandaged hand.*) That's when I broke the door down. (*Makes fist, demonstrates.*) Put my fist right through the glass!

AMELIA. What did they say? After they got up, of course.

JONATHAN. He was as cool as a surgeon. He just said, "Did you have an appointment?"

AMELIA. And she said—?

JONATHAN. "Johnny darling, you're bleeding."

AMELIA. And you said—?

JONATHAN. "You're damned right I am! But you haven't seen any real blood yet!" And I started for Fenwick. I could swear that Tina tripped me, but when I came to—while the doctor was putting on this bandage—he said I fell over a wastebasket and hit my head on a corner of his goddamned casting couch.

AMELIA. What was Tina doing—playing nurse?

JONATHAN. She was crying. She said I didn't really love her if I wouldn't let her marry Delbert.

AMELIA. And you said—?

JONATHAN. "Marry him for all I care! You and your father image. I don't want to marry my daughter —that's incest!" Isn't it?

AMELIA. The definition varies.

JONATHAN. Thank God I came to my senses in time.

AMELIA. And all it cost you was fifteen dollars. (*Looks at watch.*) Oh-oh! I'm going to miss my plane. (*Crosses to intercom.*) Julie, ask Andy to come in and help me with my luggage.

JONATHAN. Amelia, you don't understand. You can unpack. You don't have to go now. I'm back.

AMELIA. So you are. Beaten and battered, but willing to forgive and forget.

JONATHAN. I was wrong. I can't live without you.

AMELIA. Try. You don't have too many good years left.

ANDY. (*Enters, wiping off lipstick with handkerchief.*) Julie called the garage to bring your car over.

JONATHAN. (*Takes her arm.*) Amelia, don't go. I mean, don't go in that old car. (*Leads her to balcony.*) Come out here with me.

AMELIA. (*Holding back.*) I'm not interested in any double suicide pact. And you're certainly in no shape to jump alone.

JONATHAN. I want you to look at something. (*Takes her to rail, points.*) Down there. What do you see?

ANDY. Market Street.

JONATHAN. No, parked near the corner. It's your birthday present. A brand-new Jaguar.

AMELIA. (*Dryly.*) My favorite color—fuchsia.

ANDY. (*Picks up luggage.*) I'll take your bags to the car.

JONATHAN. (*Sharply.*) Put those down! (ANDY, *startled, drops them.*) Nobody carries my wife's luggage but me.

AMELIA. A one-armed redcap. This I've got to see.

ANDY. (*Sees bouquet in wastebasket.*) What happened to our flowers?

AMELIA. (*Warningly.*) Our flowers from Mr. X? Johnny brought me some others.

JONATHAN. The name is Jonathan. I never want to hear the name Johnny again.

AMELIA. All right, Johnny. Thanks for remembering my birthday, but I'm not taking you back this time.

ANDY. I'm confused. Isn't he going to marry Tina?

AMELIA. No, she's going to be Madame X.

ANDY. Mrs. Dr. Fenwick? (*Twitches in imitation.*) She swept him off his feet?

AMELIA. Literally. Jonathan, you've been the best part-time husband a woman ever had. You never forget a holiday or a birthday or an anniversary, but you never remembered to tell me how much you loved me.

JONATHAN. I do. I always have.

ANDY. I'm on his side now, Amelia. I believe him.

AMELIA. I don't. I've got enough scars already. I'll file my divorce action tomorrow. (*To* JONATHAN.) Or do you want to go ahead with yours in Reno?

JONATHAN. I just want to go home. With you.

AMELIA. The boat sailed, Jonathan. We weren't on it. (*He looks at her, realizes she means it, shrugs, and exits.*)

ANDY. (*Exasperated.*) Why? Please tell me why you wouldn't take him back?

AMELIA. Not once—not once did he say he was sorry. Or—"Amelia, forgive me." That's all I wanted to hear from him.

ANDY. (*Indicates.*) He said it when he brought you flowers.

AMELIA. Detoured from Tina to me.

ANDY. And a Jaguar!

AMELIA. No sale.

ANDY. (*Reads card in flowers.*) No sale?

AMELIA. Not to me. I'm going to be one-third of some middle-aged man's allotment in L.A. (ANDY *grins, shows her the card. She reads it.*) "Amelia, darling, I'm sorry. Forgive me."

ANDY. You can still catch him if you hurry. That Jag can do 140.

AMELIA. It's hard to drive a car when you don't have the keys.

JONATHAN. (*Enters.*) I forgot to leave you the keys.

AMELIA. (*Taking keys.*) Would you mind if I had my new car repainted?

JONATHAN. It's yours. Do any damn thing you want with it. Just drive carefully on the freeways.

AMELIA. I'll stay in the slow lane and never go over forty-five.

TINA'S VOICE. (*From outer office.*) Could I see Mrs. Bentley for a minute?

JONATHAN. It's Tina!

AMELIA. Who's Mrs. Bentley?

ANDY. You.

AMELIA. Oh, yes, of course. (JONATHAN *hurries into* ANDY'S *office but leaves door open.* TINA *does not see him as she enters.*)

TINA. (*Crosses to* AMELIA.) I don't know if you heard what happened. I'm not going to marry Johnny.

AMELIA. Really? Why not?

TINA. I'm in love with someone else. Dr. Fenwick.

AMELIA. Isn't that rather sudden?

TINA. I always fall in love suddenly. Delbert says it's a nervous condition that he can cure. I think it's called nymphomania. He's giving me a special family rate.

AMELIA. I should hope so. How did Johnny take it?

TINA. I don't enjoy seeing a man his age break down.

AMELIA. He broke down?

TINA. All he could say over and over was—"Will Amelia forgive me again?" Did I tell you I hit Johnny on the head with a paperweight—to keep him from attacking Delbert? (JONATHAN, *in doorway of* ANDY'S *office, feels the back of his head painfully.*)

AMELIA. No, you didn't.

TINA. And I want you to have this. (*Takes off ring.*) It's the engagement ring Johnny gave me.

AMELIA. Thanks. Jonathan couldn't afford one when we got married. And by the time he could, we both thought it was a foolish expenditure. I don't think so now. (*Tries on ring.*) Say, it fits! You've got chubby little fingers like mine.

TINA. Why not? We're both women.

AMELIA. Just assembled differently.

TINA. (*Offers hand.*) Thanks for everything, Miss Conway.

AMELIA. Mrs. Bentley.

DR. FENWICK. (*Twitch and tics going full blast, enters.*) Everyone's smiling. Has something gone wrong?

TINA. I was just going to thank Mrs. Bentley for bringing you into my life, darling.

DR. FENWICK. (*Embracing her.*) Wonderful girl! She's even sicker than my last wife.

AMELIA. Don't thank me. Thank Sigmund Freud. And Andy. He was low man on the couch.

TINA. (*To* DR. FENWICK.) Is it all right if I kiss Andy on the cheek?

DR. FENWICK. Be careful not to arouse his animal instincts.

TINA. Thank you, Andy. (*Kisses him on cheek.*)

ANDY. The law is just my sideline. (TINA *turns to go, sees* JONATHAN.)

JONATHAN. (*Grimly.*) Hit me with a paperweight, huh?

TINA. Forgive me, Johnny. Please?

JONATHAN. You're forgiven. You're also off salary.

TINA. Goodbye, everyone. I've been an experience, haven't I? (*She exits.*)

DR. FENWICK. You know, 1 have the feeling she's going to cure me or kill me. (*Twitches and exits.*)

AMELIA. Andy, put my luggage in the car, please. (*At look from* JONATHAN.) The *new* car. And tell Julie to start unpacking. We're not going south.

ANDY. I don't know where I'm going. Julie wants to live at my place—and I want to live at hers. Looks like we'll get it together in a Bekins moving van. (*He exits.*)

JONATHAN. Amelia, I'm afraid to ask. Am I back in the king-size bed?

AMELIA. Stop trying to read between the sheets.

JONATHAN. (*Indicates her ring.*) Now that we're engaged, where shall we go?

AMELIA. A good friend of mine owns a darling little motel just across the Bay. (*They exit arm in arm.*)

BLACKOUT—CURTAIN

*THE END*

# PROPERTY PLOT

ACT ONE, Scene 1:

*Furniture:*
   library desk, Stage Right
   bookcase, Stage Right
   waste paper basket under desk
   leather swivel chair behind desk
   swivel chair left of desk
   book-case Up Stage Right
   modern couch Stage Left
   small modern pillows on couch
   lamp on bookcase Stage Right
   lamp on small table behind couch
   small table with bric-a-brac at Downstage end of couch
   coat rack on Wall Right
   swing-out bar behind two half-doors Stage Left

*On Desk:*

   telephone with long extension cord
   ashtray
   framed picture of Jonathan
   inter-com phone
   legal pads
   pencils, miscellaneous desk paraphernalia
   file key in desk drawer

*In and On Book-Cases:*

   small tape recorder
   law books and publications
   lamp
   ashtrays
   bric-a-brac
   phone books

*On Walls:*

   diplomas
   paintings
   mirror behind couch

77

*On Bar:*

   liquor bottles and glasses

*On Shelves Behind Bar:*

   liquor bottles and glasses

*Off Left:*

   morning mail (Julie)
   briefcase     (Amelia)
   purse (Amelia)
   purse (Tina)
   purse (Mrs. Horton)
   gift-wrapped packages (Jonathan)
   gift-wrapped mink stole (Jonathan)
   bouquet of flowers (Jonathan)
   flower vases (Julie)

*Effects For All Scenes:*

   buzzer for inter-com phone
   buzzer for phone
   door opening and closing

ACT ONE, Scene 2:

*Off Right:*

   stack of law books (Andy)
   letter (Andy)

*Off Left:*

   wrapped department-store packages (Amelia)
   purse (Mrs. Horton)
   purse (Amelia)
   bank check (Julie)
   dictation pad and pencil (Julie)
   shell-rimmed glasses (Dr. Fenwick)

*Effects:*

   loud, pre-recorded snores for Dr. Fenwick

ACT ONE, Scene 3:

*On Stage:*

> morning mail on desk
> cigarettes in desk

*Off Left:*

> purse (Tina)

ACT TWO, Scene 1:

*On Stage:*

> tape recorder on desk
> cassette in box on desk
> screwdriver in desk drawer

*On Left:*

> purse (Mrs. Horton)
> purse and briefcase (Amelia)

ACT TWO, Scene 2:

*On Stage:*

> cardboard cartons
> extra law books
> two or three pieces of airline luggage
> reinforced wooden liquor box behind bar
> flowers
> vase
> card with flowers

*Off Left:*

> briefcase and purse (Amelia)
> purse (Mrs. Horton)
> car keys (Jonathan)
> flower box of birds of paradise (Jonathan)
> diamond engagement ring (Tina)
> purse (Tina)

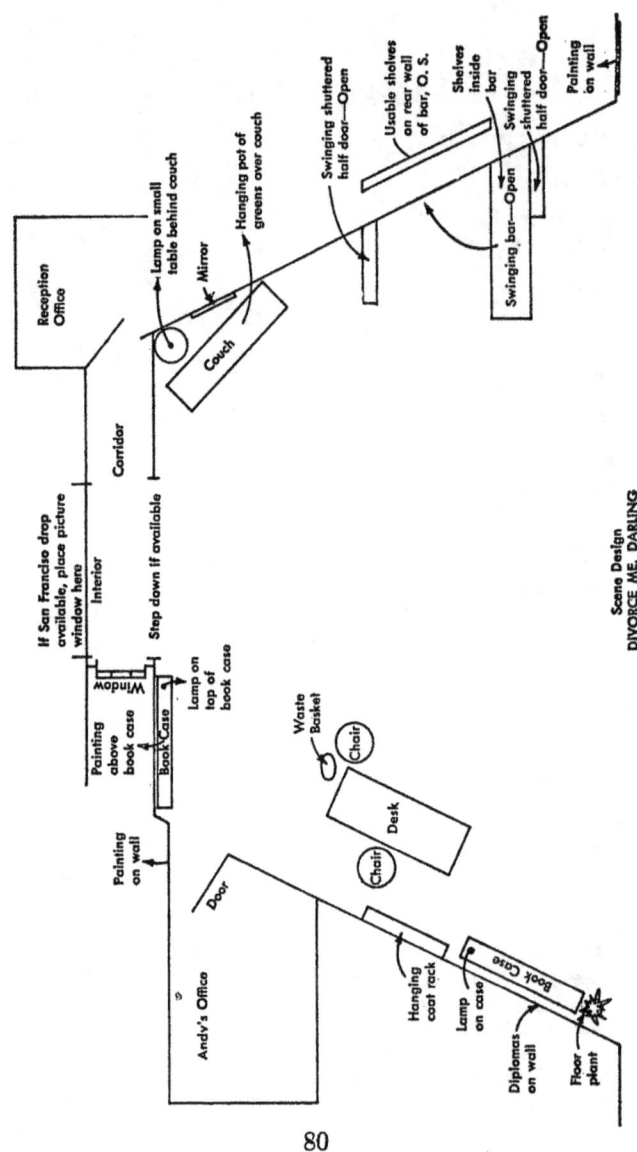

Scene Design
DIVORCE ME, DARLING

Reception Office

Lamp on small table behind couch

Mirror

Hanging pot of greens over couch

Couch

Swinging shuttered half door—Open

Usable shelves on rear wall of bar, O. S.

Shelves inside bar

Swinging shuttered half door—Open

Swinging bar—Open

Painting on wall

Corridor

Interior

If San Franciso drop available, place picture window here

Step down if available

Window

Painting above book case

Book Case

Lamp on top of book case

Waste Basket

Chair

Desk

Chair

Painting on wall

Door

Andy's Office

Hanging coat rack

Lamp on case

Book Case

Diplomas on wall

Floor plant

80

No one shall make any changes in this title(s) for the purpose of production. No part of this book may be reproduced, stored in a retrieval system, scanned, uploaded, or transmitted in any form, by any means, now known or yet to be invented, including mechanical, electronic, digital, photocopying, recording, videotaping, or otherwise, without the prior written permission of the publisher. No one shall share this title(s), or any part of this title(s), through any social media or file hosting websites.

For all inquiries regarding motion picture, television, online/digital and other media rights, please contact Concord Theatricals Corp.

## MUSIC AND THIRD PARTY MATERIALS USE NOTE

Licensees are solely responsible for obtaining formal written permission from copyright owners to use copyrighted music and/or other copyrighted third-party materials (e.g., artworks, logos) in the performance of this play and are strongly cautioned to do so. If no such permission is obtained by the licensee, then the licensee must use only original music and materials that the licensee owns and controls. Licensees are solely responsible and liable for clearances of all third-party copyrighted materials, including without limitation music, and shall indemnify the copyright owners of the play(s) and their licensing agent, Concord Theatricals Corp., against any costs, expenses, losses and liabilities arising from the use of such copyrighted third-party materials by licensees. For music, please contact the appropriate music licensing authority in your territory for the rights to any incidental music.

## IMPORTANT BILLING AND CREDIT REQUIREMENTS

If you have obtained performance rights to this title, please refer to your licensing agreement for important billing and credit requirements.